"Don't miss out on this incredible new talent."

—Love Romances & More

"A must-read." —The Road to Romance

"A gem of a tale." —Fallen Angel Reviews

"Ms. Teglia is a terrific writer who has penned a story of love and magic that left me sighing at the end."

—Just Erotic Romance Reviews

"As usual, Ms. Teglia's sex scenes were small doses of TNT and the tension was perfect." —Ecataromance.com

"I laughed, then I sighed and had tears at my eyes at the end . . . a book I intend to read again and again!"

—Joyfully Reviewed

Also by charlene Teglia

Wild Wild West
Satisfaction Guaranteed
Wicked Hot
Animal Attraction

A Shadow Guardians Novel

claimed

by the

Wolf

CHARLENE TEGLIA

St. Martin's Griffin New York

CLAIMED BY THE WOLF. Copyright © 2009 by Charlene Teglia. All rights reserved. Printed in the United States of America. For information, address St. Martin's Press, 175 Fifth Avenue, New York, N.Y. 10010.

www.stmartins.com

Library of Congress Cataloging-in-Publication Data

Teglia, Charlene.
    Claimed by the wolf : a shadow guardians novel / Charlene Teglia.—1st ed.
        p. cm.
    ISBN 978-0-312-53742-5
    1. Supernatural—Fiction.   I. Title.
    PS3620.E4357C56 2009
    813'.6—dc22

                                                2009019941

P 1

For P. with love

Acknowledgments

Thanks to the Write Ons for writing support.
And to N. J. Walters for advance reader feedback.

prologue

Kenric would have cursed when the demon he pursued evaded him, but in his wolf form he could only snarl. The sound of a wolf on the hunt denied its prey was more chilling than any curse he could have uttered, but the demon wasn't there to be intimidated by it. How could the creature have escaped him?

Frustrated fury drove him to cover the ground again, and the trail ended in the same place. A gate. The creature had fled through it to its home in the shadow realms, where Kenric could not follow. The sounds of battle forced him to turn away and abandon his hunt. This demon had fled, but the others still fought.

Kenric's pack boasted a hundred warriors at full strength. The allied forces of werewolves, witches, dragons, sidhe, vampires, and one rebel breed of demon had gathered in this ancient valley that had been home to Akkadians before the Sumerians and then Babylonians ruled. Here they made their stand against the invaders from the shadow realms.

The fight had been evenly matched when he ran after the demon. He returned to a slaughter. The air was thick with dust and the metallic tang of blood, and the bodies of the fallen covered the ground.

He understood why the tide had turned against them when he saw a witch strike down the last of his wolves while he was still too far away to assist.

Betrayed. The witches had changed their allegiance and now fought for the demons, turning on those who had trusted them enough to turn their backs.

The strike had clearly been well planned and executed. The demon he'd pursued had lured him away until it was too late. Now his pack lay butchered. His feet dug deep into shifting soil as he ran faster.

Kenric felt his muscles gather, tensing to spring. His eyes

fixed on the coven's leader. One thought consumed him; kill her and then see how well her sister witches fared.

His strength carried him through the air. His fury found its target and he brought the woman down. He saw then the reason for her perfidy, the price of the coven's loyalty. The witch clutched a spell parchment roll scribed with demon markings. Her desperate grasp became eternal as her life's blood soaked into the thirsty ground.

An unmistakable scent caught his attention. The piece of writing wasn't just inscribed by a demon, it contained potent demon magic. Kenric bit at the papyrus, determined to destroy it along with her, but it eluded him, vanishing before his jaws could close around it. The witch's now empty hand still formed a claw, as if reaching after what she had traded their world for even in death.

Death took him next.

He opened his eyes to see a woman in full battle dress, heavily armed, wings extended behind her. A star shone on her forehead. He knew who he faced. He'd seen her likeness depicted often enough.

"Inanna," he said. "What dream is this?"

"No dream." The goddess regarded him with golden eyes that burned with power. "You fought well."

"Not well enough."

"I am the judge of that."

Kenric supposed she was. Men forgot Inanna's other aspects when they celebrated her as the goddess of sexual drives. She was also a warrior goddess.

"Would you continue?"

The question made Kenric bare his teeth as if he could taste vengeance in the air. "I would continue from death and beyond. I would continue for all of eternity."

"Fierce warrior." Inanna gave him an approving smile. "You choose the same fate as your fellow captains of battle."

"They all died?" Kenric asked the question automatically, realizing as he spoke that there could have been no other outcome. The scene of slaughter he'd returned to had been too complete. Adrian, Kadar, Abaran, Ronan, were all here with him in the netherworld. Leaving the world without defense, without help or hope.

"They did. And like you, they choose to fight on. You five will wear my star and defend the world's five gates against the shadow realms. Werewolf, demon, dragon, vampire, and sidhe, you are now my chosen immortal warriors, my Shadow Guardians."

As she named him, Kenric felt fingers of fire drawing on his chest. He looked down to see her sign burned into the skin over his heart, an eight-pointed star enclosed by a circle.

one

Sybil Ames was on her way home from work when she saw the estate sale sign. The radio began to blast out Ace of Base's "The Sign" simultaneously, and it struck her as synchronicity. Estate sales had all sorts of things mixed together, trash and treasure. Lured by the possibility of a real find, she put on her blinker and pulled into the drive.

The house wasn't one of the new McMansions that seemed to be all subdivisions produced anymore. It was rickety and gloomy and more than a little surly, slanting on a hill with an aggressive tilt. If any neighborhood covenants and restrictions applied, the homeowners' association was either too apathetic or too intimidated to enforce them.

A prime location for a ghost. Sybil perked up at the possibility. She'd never encountered a real ghost. Or anything very interesting, for that matter. Her apprentice witch status pretty much made her the coven's errand girl, and everything exciting remained shrouded in secrecy. It was like being a kid who constantly heard a chorus of, "You'll understand when you're older" from the adults, but a whole lot more frustrating since she was an adult herself.

The scattered items out in the driveway were either thoroughly picked over already, or the estate hadn't had much to offer to begin with.

Picked over, Sybil decided, eyeing a piece of dark walnut furniture that had started off as quality before it wound up on the wrong side of entropy. Antique dealers tended to hit sales early and buy up anything valuable to resell.

Still, that one piece gave her hope that something else had been discarded or passed up. Her bland apartment really needed a touch of gothic. A stone gargoyle was just the sort of thing she might trip over here.

The sagging walnut armoire demanded closer inspection, so Sybil tried the doors and drawers, half-expecting a bat to fly out in the process. Instead, she found one drawer stuck tight. She pulled harder, and it came loose in a rush that almost sent

her backward. Her desperate flailing for balance wasn't graceful, but it saved her from falling on her ass. Sybil peered into
the armoire to see what caused the drawer to stick, and spotted
the book.

The leather binding was cracked and dirty. She pried it out
carefully and opened it up. It looked like a personal diary of
some sort. It wasn't. The faded words crowded the pages in a
cramped, back-slanting and almost illegible style, but the con-
tent was unmistakable.

She'd found a grimoire

Interesting. Sybil turned the brittle pages with care, slowly
deciphering handwriting the nuns at her Catholic school
would've threatened the author with hell for. Not that witches
believed in hell.

She should put it back. She held onto it anyway, reluctant
to put it down.

It looked like it contained pretty advanced magic. If she
could do a spell or two out of this book successfully, on her
own, without a senior witch overseeing every step of the ritual
and the coven approving her experiment in advance, maybe
she'd finally prove she was ready for more than sweeping up
spilled salt and washing away used pentagrams.

Maybe she could finally get a familiar of her own. Maybe
she could finally start learning something useful. Some real
magic.

She opened the book again, deliberating, and let out a startled curse when she got a paper cut on her index finger. A drop of blood fell on the book, making the decision for her. She'd damaged it, although she could argue that the book had damaged her first. Either way, she'd have to buy it now.

She tucked it under her arm and carried it with her while she poked through the remains of the estate sale. It was a disappointment, overall. No leering stone gargoyles. No buried treasure. Just trash, except for the little handwritten leather book.

Sybil made her way to the disinterested woman in charge. "How much for this?"

The woman frowned, pulled out a pair of reading glasses, and consulted a list. "Books are two dollars," she said.

Sybil paid and carted her booty home. Home was a ground-floor apartment in Oakton, Virginia, modern and comfortable and lacking in essential character. Although considering the character the estate sale house demonstrated, maybe there was something to be said for bland.

"I need a familiar," Sybil told the book. "This place needs more than a makeover. It needs life."

She put the grimoire down on her altar. It seemed like the right place for it. She felt a little shock jump from the altar's surface to her hand through the book and let out a hiss of surprise at the static discharge.

Her hand stung as if burned, then itched. Sybil rubbed it against her khakis, trying to dispel the prickling heat. She'd probably gotten fifty years' worth of dust and allergens on her skin when she picked up the book.

The explanation didn't cover the acrid scent of smoke that rose from the cover where it touched the altar. *It's just a book of shadows written in really bad cursive*, Sybil told herself. *The altar isn't rejecting it.*

Except she had cut her finger on it, and if the drop of blood had activated some long-dormant magic . . . a chill went through her and she took a step back. Her retreat came too late. The book opened, pages rifling as if turned by unseen fingers. Words glowed as if written in fire.

Sybil wanted nothing more than to rush forward and slam the book shut. Instead, she found herself moving closer as if in a trance, running her cut finger along the burning words, speaking the written words out loud. She couldn't even identify the type of spell she was compelled to recite, but the power of it was unmistakable, and it held her trapped. With each syllable, the sensation of power built. Unfortunately, it wasn't power that was hers to command. Just the opposite.

She'd wanted real magic. She realized, too late, that she should have been more specific. This was very real, and she wasn't its master. She was at its mercy.

The burning, biting itch spread from her hand up her arm,

then over her body until her entire epidermis felt like it was on fire. She said the last words of the spell in a near scream, and collapsed on her knees in relief when the prickling heat of unknown magic crawling over her skin stopped.

"Shit," she hissed. She scooted back, panting with exertion and reaction. And fear. What had she just done?

Sybil lurched upright and grabbed for salt and her athame. Make a circle. Close that thing inside it. Then call her coven and maybe an exorcist.

Her hand was shaking. She fought to steady it along with her breathing. The last thing she needed to do now was cut herself with her own ritual knife. The shaking stopped and the blade rose and swept down, slicing her other palm. Then her hand stretched out to spill more blood on the book.

"No," she growled. "No, no, no." She pulled her hand back so the red droplets sprinkled the edge of her altar instead. She watched in disbelief as the droplets moved toward the book as if pulled by some unseen source of gravity.

Not enough time to pull the altar forward and cast a circle around it. Instead, she shifted back and cast one around herself, shoving raw adrenaline into the rite to power it. Just as she was finishing, the book shot through the air and struck her chest. Then the circle rose, sealing them both inside it.

Burning, prickling heat rushed over her, and she knew the cursed thing she'd found wasn't done with her. It wanted something, and what it wanted became abruptly clear as crystal. It hungered for a conduit, a way to loose the magic it contained. And she was gifted enough but also untrained enough to be its tool.

"I won't let you use me," Sybil said through gritted teeth.

She brought her athame up to trace a protective symbol in the air. Before she finished the movement, the book pulsed against her chest like a living thing and she found her arm frozen.

She was losing.

So when the door of her apartment blew in, she welcomed the distraction. She even had a brief hope of rescue. Until a dark wolf the size of a pony came through the frame in a cloud of dust and wood fragments.

She gaped at it in astonishment. "When I said this place needed a familiar? I take it back." Her words sounded thin to her own ears.

The enormous creature saw her, crouched down, and sprang. She closed her eyes, unable to watch fanged death leaping for her. Then she remembered it couldn't reach her. But did she want it to? That was one way to break her impasse, she thought in grim determination. She swept her empty hand through the circle and broke it.

The wolf's body struck her down, knocking the book away from her in the process.

"Destroy it," she whispered as she fell under the weight of the nightmare creature, more from desperation than hope of being understood. "Burn that book of shadows and you can do whatever you want to me with my blessing."

The beast snarled something that sounded remarkably like, "Burrrrn."

Sybil turned her head to see the book on the floor beside her burst into flames that danced over the pages, crackling as they consumed. Her skin seared as if the same fire devoured her along with the paper, and she writhed in agony.

The wolf pinned her down as she burned with the book. She looked down at her bare arm to see if it was all in her mind. Symbols scored her skin. "It's writing itself on me," she whispered in horror. "Goddess save me."

The desperate plea went unanswered as far as Sybil could tell. The pain went on as waves of unknown magic buffeted and burned her. When it finally stopped, the sudden cessation was almost a new pain in itself.

She looked over at the floor where a heap of ashes should have been. Should have been, but wasn't. Her eyes flicked to the wolf that hadn't disappeared along with the book, although it had moved off of her. The ruff around its neck stood up and it didn't look friendly. From the size, it had to be a timber wolf. She couldn't imagine what it was doing in Oakton, but since it had seemed to talk, what was one more impossible thing?

She got her answer as a haze shimmered around the animal's form, distorting and obscuring it, making the limbs seem to elongate. Sybil blinked hard as the haze cleared, leaving a tall, heavily muscled naked man standing over her.

A mane of black hair fell around his shoulders. His eyes, a deep gold, pierced hers. His angular face still looked like it held a wolf's snarl. A tattoo of an odd star, like a pentagram with too many points inside a circle, decorated his chest.

He spoke in a deep growl. "Do you know what you've done, witch?"

"Asked you to burn a book," she answered, feeling numb. "I'm normally against that sort of thing, but I think this case is an exception."

His jaw tightened. "You've fed the demon spells with your blood, spoken the words that opened one of the five gates to the shadow realms, alerted any forces still seeking it that the lost book has been found, and shot up magic flares to pinpoint its location."

"You forgot the part where I broke my protective circle so you could rip me to pieces as long as you got the book, too." She rubbed her arms, now once again bare of any marking. "And by the way, I take back what I said about doing anything you want with me, since you didn't do your part."

She thought she saw a muscle over his eye twitch. "If you

hadn't already joined your blood to demon magic, it could not have transferred itself from that body to yours."

Her jaw sagged. "What? Are you saying I'm possessed?" The full horror of it struck her. "They're in me. All those words. Those incantations want to be spoken. They want to use me to do it." Sybil stared at the stranger in front of her, appalled. "Stop me. Whatever that book of shadows is, it's evil. Stop me before it makes me do anything else."

"I would love nothing more." He glared at her. "But you begged the goddess for aid, and she's chosen to grant it."

TWO

Sybil stared at the stranger. "What would you know about an answer to prayer? Weren't you a wolf when you came in?"

His lips tightened. They were very well-shaped lips, and in other circumstances she would have appreciated that a lot more. He didn't answer, and she supposed she couldn't really expect him to.

She looked around her living room and wondered why it looked so normal after everything that had just happened. With one notable exception. "You broke my front door," she said. "There goes my damage deposit."

He turned toward it, touched the tattoo on his chest, and Sybil heard a soft whoosh and felt her ears pop as the pressure in the room abruptly shifted. The door became solid again. She blinked, then got up, and went over to touch it. It felt as real as it looked.

"Thanks."

"We will erase as many signs of what went on here as we can." His hard tone made it clear that he wasn't doing her any favors. He had his own agenda and this just happened to fit in it.

Sybil nodded. Then frowned. "Um, how?"

"It's a simple spell, elementary magic. You are a witch, aren't you?"

"Yes and no." Sybil blew out a breath, shooting a stray lock of hair out of her eyes in the process. "I'm an apprentice."

"Apprentice." He gave her a skeptical look. "You don't look like a child."

"I'm an adult. They just haven't taught me much."

"They?"

"My coven. They let me join because, well, it's hereditary."

"Hereditary."

Sybil blew her hair back again with a short huff. "Are you going to just stand there repeating everything I say while we wait to see if I'm going to spontaneously combust?"

"Do you think you might?"

He said it so deadpan, Sybil felt her heart jump. "Is that a real possibility?"

"With demon magic, anything is possible." He looked her over intently. "Explain why you are a hereditary witch with no training."

"It's not because my coven's lazy or incompetent," Sybil said, feeling defensive. "It's just that they think if I don't know anything, I can't do any harm. Also, if I'm an active member of the coven with apprentice status, they can keep an eye on me."

The man-wolf tilted his head as he considered her. "Why would they fear you'd do harm?"

"Prophecy," Sybil said bluntly. "It's dumb. Way back in ancient history somebody prophesied that a witch of my line is supposed to end the world. So all of us, generation after generation, get brought into the coven and stuck with doing errands and odd jobs. It's a complete waste of talent."

"And yet here you are, the holder of ancient demon magic many would kill to possess."

Sybil swallowed hard. "Are you saying I'm going to destroy the world because a book I bought at a yard sale made me?" If she'd heard a wild statement like that this morning, she would have laughed. Now it didn't seem funny.

"I won't let you."

"That sounds ominous." She rubbed her arms, remembering

the spells searing their way into her. "I don't suppose you'd like to tell me why you came bursting in here in the first place?"

"You opened a gate to the shadow realms," he answered. "I guard those gates."

"It made me say a spell," Sybil said. "Is that what opened the gate?"

"Yes. And that particular spell could only have come from the lost book. It was simple to trace the magic to its source and find you."

"Simple for anybody besides you?" Sybil asked the question in a small voice.

"If any others have been watching for the book, they know where to find it now."

"Right." She tried not to hyperventilate, wondering what else could come through her door that would be worse than a timber wolf. The man-wolf took her elbow. She started at the contact.

"Time to go," he said.

"Right. I'm just trying to think where."

"Where is not up to you."

Before she could argue, some sort of mist swirled around both of them. When it cleared, her apartment was gone. Oakton was gone. She stared around at what looked very much like a desert and asked the obvious question. "Where are we?"

. . .

Kenric released the witch he'd taken in tow and resisted the urge to curse. Not only was she a witch, she had the book in her possession. Or rather, it possessed her. The distinction might have made her innocent of knowingly opening the gate, but it made her no less a threat.

His fellow guardians had gone after creatures who had taken advantage of the opening to enter the mortal world. He had gone after the one who made the opening. After all this time, the demon book had finally reappeared. At last it could be destroyed, the threat it posed ended.

But the thing had eluded him, slipping from his grasp and hiding in the lithe body of the witch. As if the witch wasn't already dangerous enough without it.

He took a moment to study the source of his frustration. She was interesting to look at, arresting rather than pretty. Even without the invisible nimbus of power that crackled around her, she had a presence that attracted attention. What would his fellow guardians make of her?

She was tall and slender, with hair streaked in shades of sun and sand that fell in locks and whorls around her face. One seemed determined to cover her left eye, leaving him looking at one blue orb and three quarters of her features, including an upturned nose and a pointed chin beneath full lips settled in a stubborn line.

"Not answering?" Her well-shaped mouth moved as he watched. Her face was mobile and expressive, and her brain seemed to jump topics faster than a rabbit. "Okay, next question. How'd you turn into a wolf?"

"The usual way," he said.

She ran blunt-nailed fingers through her hair. "The usual way. Right. I suppose if you told me, you'd have to kill me. Can you at least tell me your name?"

"Kenric."

"Kenric." She repeated it, tilting her chin to look up at him. She wasn't petite, but he stood a head above her. "I'm Sybil."

The words hung for a moment as if she was waiting for a response. When she didn't get one, she moved on. "So, now I have this thing inside me." She shuddered, then wrapped her arms around her middle. "How do we get it out?"

"Why do you assume I'll help you?"

She shrugged, narrow shoulders rising and falling. "You didn't bring me along with you out of a desperate need for feminine companionship. You seem to know a lot more than I do, and you broke my door to come after it, not me. I'm sure you have your own agenda, but when it comes to the book, you want it and I don't. I'd say we share a common goal."

"How do you know I don't just want to use it, or you?"

"If you'd wanted to use it, you could have just grabbed it and ran when I opened the circle."

"Maybe I'm trying to keep you off balance," Kenric said.

"Don't think so." She seemed unconcerned. "Is there an oasis around here?"

"Yes." He indicated the right direction. She started off. He followed. Barely a moment passed before her voice trailed back to him.

"Not that I'm complaining about the view, but aren't you worried about getting sunburned in awkward places?"

"No."

"A man of few words. Or are you actually a wolf?"

"Keep walking."

She sighed and did so. He didn't expect her silence to last long. He could practically feel more questions pulsing from her. But she managed to stay quiet until they climbed a rise and the oasis came into view below.

"Oh. Pretty!" Her pace quickened, although her feet sank and slid in the sand.

He supposed it was. The small body of water sparkled in the sun, the deep blue providing striking contrast to the wild-flowers, juniper, and acacia growing around the water's edge. A red-tailed hawk circled overhead, seeking prey. Kenric envied it. The hawk's hunt would end in satisfaction.

He watched the woman in front of him skirt around native plants until she found a rock outcropping to perch on.

"This is great." She waved an enthusiastic hand. "I had no idea there was so much life in the desert."

"There is life everywhere."

"Well, yeah, I guess." She drew her knees up and rested her pointed chin on them. "It's just that I thought it would be all empty sand. It isn't. Lots of different kinds of plants. Animal burrows."

"Noisy witches."

She gave him a look that was somewhat hampered by the hair over her eye. "You, of course, have no flaws."

He responded with silence.

"So, are you a lycan . . . a werewolf?"

If he was a wolf, she'd stop pelting him with questions. Kenric let action follow thought and shifted form.

"I'll take that as a yes." She leaned back to watch the hawk.

The mixed scents of animals and plants exploded around him, tinged with the smells of water and earth. Overlaying everything was the distinctive perfume of witch and woman, redolent with herbs and magic.

Breathing her in was worse than talking to her. The inescapable essence of female assaulted his nose. He'd been aware enough of her as a man. As a wolf, his senses took in even more detail. That heightened awareness would carry over when he shifted again. He didn't want to think of her as anything but the obstacle that stood between him and his prey, that damned book that had escaped him twice.

Annoyed, he turned away to catch the trail of a rabbit.

sybil followed the flight of a bird and wondered what it had spotted. A mouse? She imagined the sharp eyes, the patient waiting rewarded with opportunity, the dive, talons outstretched.

Her sympathies were with the mouse. She felt small and vulnerable, exposed and defenseless. If the wolf was right, something like the bird of prey could be watching her now. Or would be soon. At any moment, an unknown magical predator could sight her.

The prophecy she'd once considered ridiculous and alarmist now seemed a lot more serious. If she allowed destructive power to fall into the wrong hands, wouldn't it be her fault if it got used?

Today's events didn't change her mind about her determination to learn. The coven was still wrong. If she'd had more training, she might have recognized the book of shadows for what it was. She'd have known demonic work when she tripped over it. She might have been able to defend herself. Instead, her lack of knowledge and experience made her the perfect tool. She had enough latent power to perform demon magic without the skills that might have made her the master of it instead of the victim.

If the coven had planned it for centuries, they couldn't have come up with a better way to make that prophecy a reality. The irony of it made Sybil want to groan out loud.

She glanced over at the huge wolf. It didn't look any less intimidating on further acquaintance. Kenric was sniffing the air, his stance alert. She wondered if he sensed danger, and how much of a danger he posed himself.

At least he'd taken her into the middle of nowhere. It suited her to be far away from a population center. She felt like a ticking bomb. The further away she was from people, the fewer she could hurt. If Kenric was telling her the truth, she'd already endangered the world by opening a gate that should have stayed closed.

Thinking about that made anxiety rise, bringing with it a sick wave of heat. She closed her eyes and tried to control her breathing, to relax, to not panic. But instead of dissipating, the heat became a fever that pulsed through her. The memory of seeing symbols branded into her skin made her eyes fly open. She raised her arms, frantically checking to see if she was displaying a spell.

Nothing marred her bare arms. Except a red flush she hadn't been in the sun long enough to warrant. The heat grew more intense and Sybil shuddered, then gasped as flame engulfed her arms.

"Help! Fire!" She threw herself off the rock outcropping and dropped into the sand, rolling as she shouted the words. But stop, drop, and roll didn't have the desired effect. She kept rolling until she hit the water's edge and plunged her arms in, hoping nothing dangerous lurked under the surface. Instead of feeling a soothing cool, the sensation of heat intensified. She pulled her arms back out and stared at the fire licking her skin.

Male hands settled on her shoulders and moved down, smoothing away the flame. Or maybe just coaxing it back below the surface; she felt like a glowing stove full of banked coals. His hands stopped when they covered hers, exerting a light pressure that felt comforting.

"All right?"

The deep voice spoke near her ear. Kenric was right behind her, a man once again and wearing only skin. He might be a wolf, but he was all male. The knowledge sent a shiver of awareness through her.

"Um," she managed. "Maybe spontaneous combustion isn't off the table."

"You didn't combust. You're not burned."

Now that he pointed it out, Sybil realized he was right. "It feels like I'm burning inside," she said. "Like a fever."

Kenric's hands stroked their way back up to her shoulders,

then down again. She made a restless movement in an attempt to shrug off the prickles of heat and rubbed herself against his naked torso in the process. It felt far too good.

"Ah. Sorry," she muttered.

"Does it help to move?"

"Yes. No." Sybil frowned and tried hard to stay still. The urge to slide back and press closer to him seemed a lot more likely to scorch her than phantom fire.

"Which?"

She blew out a breath, dislodging the curl that always fell over her eye. "Neither. You should probably let go of me."

His hands tightened on her. "Should I?"

"Look, this is embarrassing, but you're making me hotter." The blunt words were out before she could think better of it.

"Hotter." He sounded thoughtful. Hands caressed her arms, making her incredibly aware of the sensitive inner hollows at her wrists and elbows, and sending a different heat flaring.

"Yes." The word came out nearly in a pant.

"Then it may be best to fight fire with fire. You need a focus and a release."

He was so not helping. Sybil closed her eyes and fought to keep from flinging herself at him. That became much more difficult when his hands skated along her shoulders and down the front of her until his fingertips brushed the upper swells of her breasts. The sleeveless top she wore didn't seem like much of a barrier. The flimsy bra underneath was more of a seductive tease than a shield for modesty.

"This is a bad idea," Sybil said.

"Because I'm a werewolf?"

She arched her back to thrust herself into his hands. "I was thinking more because we can't really trust each other and you might have to kill me to destroy the book."

He caressed her breasts and teased her nipples with his palms. "Trust isn't necessary for this."

The intimate contact made her crave more. The need for release had never felt more urgent. And it wasn't like they had a better option. Sybil surrendered to the moment and fed the heat inside her into his touch.

Three

ighting fire with fire wasn't cooling her off, so Sybil reached down and grabbed the hem of her shirt, pulling it up. Kenric helped and between the two of them they bared her torso except for her sheer scrap of a bra. It wasn't much, but the small triangles of fabric trapped heat against her skin so she fumbled for the front clasp and sighed with relief when it opened.

"Small," Kenric muttered, tracing the underside of her breasts with his fingers.

"Maybe, but right now they're naked," Sybil said. The words came out in a low, throaty tone.

"Observation. Not complaint or comparison." Clever hands found nerve endings and played them to blistering effect.

"Whatever." She turned to face him and caught sight of his penis, now fully erect and taut against his belly. "You're not disinterested." More heat kindled inside her and flared out. She pressed her body into his, willing to let him smother the fire with bare flesh.

His hands closed on her waist, pulling her closer. "I'm male. You're female."

"You noticed that? I did, too." She arched her back, enjoying the sensation of his muscled flesh against her naked breasts.

"I noticed you have more on than me."

"Hmm, you're right. That doesn't seem fair."

Kenric's grip shifted as he lowered her onto her back beside the water. Fingers found the snap and zip at the waistband of her khakis, opened both. The air that touched her exposed belly did nothing to cool her down.

One thought, however, did.

"Is this another spell taking over?" Sybil stared at Kenric, alarmed by the possibility because even if it was, she didn't think she could stop. He didn't seem inclined to, either.

"It's energy seeking an outlet," he answered. "Better to give it one of your choosing than risk it taking the path of least resistance."

She raised a brow at him. "I'm not feeling much resistance here."

"Good." He lowered his head to her and Sybil sighed in pleasure as she felt his lips skim the valley between her breasts. Nice, but . . .

"Your aim is off."

"My aim is perfect." He continued downward in a straight path, his breath sending shivers of delight through her as it tantalized her bare skin. A smile tugged at her lips as she realized he was right. As much as she'd like to have his mouth exploring her upper curves, she was half-crazed to feel it right where he was heading.

When he reached her navel, the tip of his tongue teased the sensitive recess. Hidden nerve endings sparked to life. The wicked caress made her hips move in silent urging as desire for more burned hotter.

He worked her pants down her hips with her enthusiastic cooperation, then leaned back and pulled until they reached her ankles. She quivered as his fingers followed the lower edge of her panties from her hips to her inner thighs. The tips of his fingers slid underneath the fabric, and she groaned as she felt him brush so close to her sex that anticipation made her jerk.

It was crazy. She didn't know him, didn't know where they were, who might be watching. And she didn't care. The sand underneath her felt cool against her heated skin, and the friction it created when she moved amplified her reaction, adding another frisson of stimulation.

If anything could take her mind off the fact that she was currently possessed and a real threat to herself and others, a good orgasm ranked right up with a bomb going off for distraction quotient. Also, if the conflagration under her skin was energy seeking an outlet, an orgasm seemed like the safest channel.

Saved by sex, she thought, and then stopped thinking as his hands moved to the insides of her knees and pressed out, making an open diamond of her legs.

His hands stayed where they were, drawing patterns on her thighs that made her quiver. His mouth moved a breath away from the thin fabric covering her mound. When he exhaled, the warmth touched her in a phantom caress. Then his lips followed, lightly tracing her folds, before he pressed a harder kiss at her center.

She made a low sound of encouragement and wound her fingers into his hair.

He moved up until his teeth caught the upper band of her panties and peeled them down just far enough to expose her. Then his lips found her clit, and Sybil groaned at the intimate contact that incited sensitive nerve endings. His tongue laved the distended nub, and it was almost too much. Her hips rocked up in response. He licked down and dipped the tip of his tongue into her core, and Sybil felt like a volcano on the verge of eruption.

"Yes, yes, yes," she muttered, "There. Oh, yes."

She felt his tongue penetrating her further, moving inside her, his mouth devouring her. When he stroked a fingertip over the slick hood of her clitoris, pleasure built to the breaking point. His fingertip and his mouth found a rhythm that made her blood pound, as if her heart had escalated to match. Her sex pulsed, echoing the beat, and she came in a rush. The intensity of release pulled her muscles taut and she nearly came up off the ground.

Afterward, she panted and tried to get her bearings. "Thanks," she finally said.

For an answer, Kenric tugged her panties back up. That was probably the right thing to do, but it didn't stop a tinge of disappointment from coloring her afterglow. She reached down to pull her khakis on before he could do that, too, needing to at least pretend she was in control of something in her world.

She risked a look at him from under her lashes, and noticed his cock still standing at full attention.

"Um."

His eyes followed the direction of her gaze. "Yes?"

"Do you want, you know, ah. Should I return the favor?"

"Not now."

She blinked. "You're taking a rain check on a blowjob? Now I know you're not human."

He bared his teeth at her. Sybil decided to take that as humor and not threat. Especially since she wasn't really in any condition to run if he wasn't kidding around. Her legs felt like spaghetti and she was already breathing like she'd finished a hard sprint.

She looked away, since that seemed like the safest response, and stood to finish buttoning and zipping herself back together.

Then she looked around at the desert flora, the water, the view in the distance, anywhere but at the aloof stranger who'd just gone down on her.

"Is it getting dark?" Sybil finally asked when she couldn't stand the silence any longer. It should be if they were still on the same side of the planet; she'd stopped at the estate sale on her way home from work, and while events had moved at a breakneck pace since, it still had to be late evening. The thought that so little real time had elapsed was a little disorienting.

"Yes."

"Are we spending the night here?"

"No."

"Should we be walking, then?"

"Not necessary."

Well, okay. Sybil tipped her head back to watch as the first pale stars appeared. It comforted her that some things remained constant. The sun still set in the west, stars still shone, the world continued to spin on its axis. It made her feel hopeful.

Ghost flames danced across her vision, then winked out. She frowned. "Tell me about the book."

"It's the work of chaos demons."

"How could it write itself onto me? Into me?"

"The book was a merely a container for the spells to inhabit. The spells *are* the magic."

Sybil turned to look at Kenric, careful to keep her eyes on his and not on anything more distracting. "How can magic just be made of words?"

"Words are power. I know you're untrained, but surely you know that much."

"Well, yeah. But they're not alive."

"Aren't they?" His expression seemed serious. Sybil felt her throat constrict.

"No," she said firmly.

"As you say."

She scuffed the toe of her shoe against the ground. "Okay, fine, words are alive and these particular words came from chaos demons. Why did the book get written in the first place?"

Kenric's face hardened. "Witches made a bargain. Long

ago. The word of unmaking would have been spoken and chaos would have been let loose."

"Would have been." She pounced on that point. "Let's come back to that, but first, what is the word of unmaking?"

"The lost word." He gave her the sort of look a teacher might direct at a problem student. "Creation came into being with a word. The lost word unmakes."

"Genesis and its opposite. Huh. Okay." This conversation was making her head throb. The idea that a single word could undo everything, and that it was currently inside her, was enough to bring on a killer migraine. "So way back in history, some witches made a deal to get the lost word and turn everything into chaos. Their plans went wrong, and ever since it's just been hiding out in a book until I found it and bled on it?"

"It hid in many places and forms over the centuries, but yes."

"Peachy." Her sour tone said volumes. No wonder nobody would train her. She could destroy the world by going shopping.

The sound of wings overhead gave her something else to think about. She watched as a large bird headed toward them through the deepening dusk. Something about the shape was odd, and as it came closer she realized it was big. Really big. With a really long neck. More like a flying lizard than any bird . . .

She took an involuntary step closer to Kenric as her eyes translated the image to her brain. "Did it see us? Is it too late to run?"

"Much too late." He sounded more resigned than alarmed as the dragon swooped down on them and backwinged to perform a neat landing.

Sybil let out a yelp and dove behind Kenric. "What do we do now?"

"We get on." He strode toward the dragon, which had curled itself into an obliging position, and climbed up to sit between the wings.

"Thanks, I'll walk." Sybil backed away.

"Get on." The dragon and the man spoke in unison, bringing her up short.

Talking dragons. Talking wolves who turned into men with amazing oral talents. Living books. Afraid to ask what was next, Sybil took a hesitant step toward the bronze-colored winged beast.

It lowered its head as if offering a confidence. "I am a vegetarian," it rumbled.

"Of course you are."

Kenric stretched out his hand to grab hers and haul her up. She straddled the beast's back behind him, wrapped her arms around his waist, and clung tight.

"Ready," Kenric said.

Wings extended with a sound like a parachute engaging. Sybil closed her eyes and tried to pretend she was riding a motorcycle. Her stomach plummeted as the ground fell away beneath them.

"You can let go now." Kenric's voice was level, not raised in a shout in order to be heard over the rush of wind and wings.

Sybil let her grip loosen slightly and peeked down. Oh, good. It was over. She released him and jumped off the dragon so fast she almost fell on her face. A long, pointed tail curled around her waist and righted her. She let out a startled shriek.

"Vegetarian," the dragon repeated.

"Right. Um, thanks." She touched the scaly tail with a tentative hand. It felt warmer than she expected, same as the beast's back and sides. Weren't reptiles cold-blooded?

"Anytime." The tail squeezed, then released her in a leisurely slide that felt like a caress. Was the creature flirting with her? She shook her head to clear the thought.

It was ridiculous. Even if it was flirting, human and dragon couldn't possibly have compatible parts. She imagined it, anyway, the dragon stalking toward its helpless, chained prey, sending its triangular-tipped tail under a skirt to twine around a feminine thigh. . . .

"Don't stop, this is getting good," the dragon said.

She jumped. It couldn't read her thoughts. Could it?

"That would be rude."

"Crap." Sybil felt a wave of heat rush to her cheeks. "Sorry. Vivid imagination. Didn't mean to offend."

"I find your thoughts entertaining. Feel free to continue. Does the beast tear her dress off with his sharp talons next?"

Kenric turned to stare at her.

"Shut up," she hissed.

"Maybe it runs one claw down the middle of her gown, cutting it open and exposing her naked flesh to its lusting gaze," the creature mused.

"Quit toying with the witch," Kenric said.

"She started it."

"I did not," Sybil snapped. "You started it by flirting with me."

"You're the one with the vivid imagination."

She blew out a breath. "Fine. You were still flirting with me, and don't try to say you weren't."

"Of course I was. You smell delectably female."

The matter of fact tone made her want to scream. Of course dragons flirted. Of course they went around offering rides and listening to private thoughts and interjecting inflammatory comments.

"Moving on," she said, trying to recover a shred of dignity.

"With pleasure. There you are, helpless and mostly naked,

my tail twined around your bare thigh, trembling with anticipation. . . ."

"Enough," Kenric interrupted. "See to her. I want to hear what news the others have." He strode off, leaving Sybil alone with a dragon who had a warped sense of humor.

"You weren't lying about being a vegetarian, were you?" Apprehension colored her voice and she cast a nervous look after Kenric's retreating back. His bare backside made a welcome distraction.

"If I'm not, you'd better find another way to distract me." The creature curled on its side, making itself comfortable. The tail curved around the hind limbs, catlike. One foreclaw patted the ground in invitation. "Come. Sit."

Sybil took the indicated spot. If it wanted to pounce on her, it would. She couldn't hope to evade or outrun it.

"That's right, little girl, the fearsome beast is inescapable. So come cuddle up."

She felt the foreclaw rake through her hair. Then the short limb nudged her shoulder, silently directing her to lean back against its chest. "Just don't breathe fire on me," she muttered as she settled into a surprisingly comfortable pose between the beast's front limbs. "I've had enough of that for one day."

"Wouldn't dream of it." The creature nuzzled the curve of her neck, making her jump. "Tense, aren't you? And after our friend the wolf did so much to relax you."

charlene Teglia

Sybil closed her eyes. "I don't want to know how you know that."

"It didn't take a mind-reader. I could smell you on him a mile away. Although his mind did have some fascinating pictures. You made quite an impression on him. He doesn't usually project so strongly."

"I said I didn't want to know." Her voice turned sharp and she felt her body stiffen defensively. "And it's none of your business. Also, he wasn't a wolf at the time, so don't think I do animals."

"And yet you have such interesting ideas about dragons and their helpless female captives." The voice resonated in its chest, deepening the tone.

"That's me. Full of interesting ideas."

"Full of questions, too. You want to know where we are. The answer is Xanadu."

And she'd thought she was numb to further surprises. "As in, where Alph, the sacred river, ran down to a sunless sea?" She scanned their surroundings, recalling the mystical realm described by romantic poet Samuel Taylor Coleridge in his immortal poem. Scholars attributed the vision to an opium-induced dream, but now Sybil had to wonder.

"It's not entirely sunless." The dragon continued, "Poetic license. Also, Coleridge was on drugs when he wrote that."

A short laugh escaped her. "What about the ice caverns? Did he get that right?"

"He did. You'll see for yourself. Later. Meanwhile, relax and enjoy my company and I'll answer more of your questions."

"Really? Let's start with an easy one. Who are you?"

four

Kadar. It means powerful."

"Well, that fits," Sybil said.

"Thank you."

She could practically hear it preening. "Is it hard to fly carrying that ego?"

"It's not as much of a burden as my huge member."

She laughed and felt tension ease in her shoulders. "Oh, yes. All the better to terrify helpless maidens with."

"Not terrify. Impress."

"If you're trying to side-track me so I won't ask more questions, you're doomed to failure," Sybil said, still grinning. "Kenric told me he guarded the gate I accidentally opened. Is that what you do, too? Are you guys some sort of paranormal police force? And are there more of you?"

"Yes, not precisely, and yes," Kadar answered. "We don't attempt to police all supernatural activity. We have a much narrower jurisdiction. Our task is to guard the gates to the world from the shadow realms."

"Set a thief to catch a thief," Sybil mused out loud. "Or in this case, set supernatural creatures to keep the world safe for humanity. So far we have a surly werewolf and a wise-ass dragon. I can hardly wait to see what the others are."

"I'll enjoy watching your reaction when you do," Kadar said.

"I'll bet." Sybil sighed and breathed in the warm, slightly spicy, and surprisingly pleasant scent of dragon.

"Thank you. You smell good, too." The triangular head rubbed against hers.

"Yeah, especially with ketchup."

"I wouldn't eat you. Unless you wanted me to. You didn't object to the wolf's attentions."

She heard laughter in the beast's low-pitched voice and resisted the urge to respond with a sharp elbow. "He didn't have scales and a tail."

"You don't know what you're missing," Kadar sighed as if mourning lost opportunity. "My tongue is forked. Imagine the possibilities."

"I'm trying not to," she murmured. "This is obscene."

"No, this is tension relief. I want you relaxed. When you tense up, your body temperature skyrockets."

"It does?" Apprehension made her tense despite the warning. It hurt to burn.

"Yes. Breathe out slowly and think of maidens chained to rocks."

She closed her eyes and tried to picture it, but the memory of her arms sheathed in flame overrode her attempts. "Kadar, what if I go all fiery again? Maybe I should move away."

"I'm scorch-proof. Now, focus. Maiden. Rock. Chains. Gown in shreds. No underwear."

"It's not working." Her breathing hitched as heat built under her skin.

"Quivering with fear. Or is it excitement?" Kadar mused.

"Kadar."

"Definitely excitement. The dragon is irresistible."

"The dragon is relentless," she shot back, but the heat ebbed. She sagged in relief.

"Dragons are wise. All the legends agree," Kadar said, his tone smug. "Now enjoy the moment. It's a beautiful evening. Count the stars as they rise."

"Okay." Sybil counted until she lost her place completely, but it didn't matter. The calming task did its job, even if she kept recounting the same points of light. She caught the motion of a shooting star from the corner of one eye, and turned to look, watching the trail cross the expanse of sky and disappear.

Ripples of color washed across the night, and she gasped out loud. "What's that?"

"Northern lights."

"Wow." She took in the show in silent awe, almost holding her breath. When the dancing colors faded from the sky, she looked back in the direction Kenric had gone and found an even more impressive sight.

Four men strode toward her. At least, she thought they were men. Considering the dragon she was using as a backrest and the werewolf she'd already met, what were the odds that the other three walking beside Kenric were human?

Not very, Sybil decided. But when they looked that good, who cared?

One was taller than the werewolf's human form, although none of them were short. The taller one had long, silver hair that gleamed in the moonlight. The next man's hair was as dark as Kenric's, although worn shorter, and they were nearly matched for height. Kenric's body seemed more heavily muscled and slightly broader in contrast. The fourth man had dark skin and a beautifully defined body that looked almost sculpted. His head was entirely bald, and on him it looked dangerously good.

Vin Diesel on steroids, she thought, playing a really hot, really bad guy.

They were all bare to the waist, hips and legs encased in some tight, form-fitting material. Leather, maybe? Kenric looked even more exotic standing with them. Wilder. More untamed.

"This is like goth porn," Sybil said out loud. Behind her, the dragon snickered.

"I am Abaran," the dark-skinned man said with some exotic accent she couldn't place, in a tone that promised wicked things. His voice made gooseflesh dance over her skin.

"Adrian." The man next to Kenric whose dark hair was cropped short spoke next, his voice hard and almost curt.

"Ronan." The tallest spoke last, and something in his voice made Sybil press closer to Kadar.

"Smart girl," Kadar murmured. "He plays rough."

"Something tells me all of you do," Sybil said. She took a good look at the four men who now ranged in front of her. Each of them had the eight-pointed star set in a circle tattooed on their chests. She recognized it finally. Inanna's star, the precursor to the present-day pentagram. What did it mean?

She turned to take a closer look at Kadar.

He obligingly raised himself up. "Want to see mine?"

"Yes." She ignored the obvious double meaning and waited. A haze formed around him that shouldn't have surprised her. It faded away to reveal another naked man with a tattoo to match the others. His hair was the same shade of bronze his hide had been, his eyes a deep, jeweled green.

"You like?" Kadar posed for her, flexing his muscles and showing off. His thick penis hung down his thigh, and Sybil noted that it wasn't engorged. What did it look like when he was aroused? Then she noticed the ridged, bumpy flesh surrounding the base with thick spines reminiscent of a sea urchin and gulped.

"Told you I had a huge member," Kadar murmured, grinning at her. His teeth flashed white and sharp in the moonlight.

"Very impressive," she assured him.

"Enough clowning." Kenric made a sharp gesture at Kadar. "We have decided what is to be done with you, witch."

"I'm all ears." Sybil fought to sound calm.

"You threw yourself on Inanna's mercy. She wishes to grant it. Therefore, we are agreed. You will accept her mark and serve her."

"Let me think," she said. "Is it better to be at the mercy of a goddess, or demonic spells bent on turning the world into chaos? Kind of a no-brainer. I accept."

"You should hear the terms first," Kadar said. His grin widened with a humor she found alarming.

"Fine. Tell me the terms." She sat straighter and folded her hands in her lap.

"Transference of her mark and her power can only come by way of her chosen."

Kenric made the statement as if it should make sense. Sybil's brow furrowed. "Huh?"

"He means the five of us," Kadar said. "We are Inanna's chosen, the Shadow Guardians entrusted with the mark of her power and bound to use it in her service."

"Okay. Fine. Transfer the mark." Sybil stood up and brushed herself off. "I'm ready."

"Are you?" The tallest one, Ronan, asked the question.

"Don't sound so eager," Abaran said. "You're last. If you damage her, we don't have time to wait for her recovery."

That sounded bad. "How, exactly, is the mark transferred?" Sybil's mouth went dry as she waited for further explanation.

"I told you. By the five of us." Kadar moved closer and stroked her arm with a knowing touch. "You will go to each of our beds in turn, and we will mark you."

Her jaw went slack for a speechless minute. "You mean, I'm supposed to have sex with all of you?"

"Yes." He read her thoughts and chuckled. "She is a sex goddess. What did you expect?"

"I thought it was just, you know, like getting a tattoo." Although she should've known better. It couldn't be anything so simple. Something so permanent would mean ritual magic. Sex magic made perfect sense, given whose power she'd be taking.

"It is not made of ink," Kenric broke in. "It is a living mark, not merely an emblem of the goddess's power. It is her power conferred. Accepting the mark will give you power to control the demon magic inside you, and to undo its work. You will be able to close the gate you opened."

"Ah." She nodded slowly. "That would be good."

"We'll be good, too," Kadar purred.

"I'm sure." Actually, she didn't doubt that the sex would be mind-blowing, considering the taste Kenric had given her. Or she'd given him. Whatever. Still . . . "Isn't there another way?"

Kenric shook his head. "Not to transfer the mark to one living. She marked each of us with raw power in the netherworld, then returned us to life. Such direct transference isn't an option for you."

Sybil swallowed. Their deaths had provided the means for their marks. Sex magic beat death magic if she had to choose which way to power the ritual. "Will it hurt?"

"She's the goddess of sex and war," Kenric stated.

"Yeah, that's not exactly an answer." She looked at Ronan. "Why'd Abaran say you might damage me? Are you a sadist?"

"I long to punish you." He sounded utterly sincere and terrifyingly intent. His pale blue eyes lit up, and his lips curved with sensual cruelty.

"Sounds like pain to me." She turned back to face Kenric, ignoring the way Kadar was toying with her hair. "How much is it going to hurt?"

"Compared to taking demon magic inside yourself?" He raised a brow as if to underscore his point, then continued, "I took the mark after death. You are living. So I can't say what you'll feel, but I don't imagine it could be worse then what you've already endured."

"Right." She wrapped her arms around herself, shivering at the memory. Well, she'd survived that. She'd survived ghost fire eating at her skin without consuming her. So, what was a little sex in comparison?

"Not a little," Kadar murmured, correcting her thought. His hands closed over her shoulders and he pulled her back against his chest, letting her feel his growing arousal. "You will belong to each of us for a full day and night to satisfy our needs."

"Okay, more than a little sex," Sybil said out loud. "Five days. Five nights." With five supernatural men, all stunning in their own way. How bad could it be?

"You will soon find out how it will be," Kadar said, stroking the skin at the base of her throat with one thumb she could all too easily imagine as a claw. "You will be chained to a rock inside my cavern and we will see if you are sufficient to appease my appetite."

She had no answer to that. Her eyes went to Kenric's. "Kadar wants me to play dragon sacrifice. Ronan wants to punish me. What do you want?"

He didn't answer, just stared unblinking at her, sexual intent gleaming in his golden eyes. The loaded silence should have alarmed her, but the memory of his mouth on her brought a shiver of sensual anticipation instead.

"What about you?" She looked to Abaran next, taking her eyes off Kenric with an effort.

"I'm a demon. I crave human." His black eyes glittered with a hunger that made her stomach knot.

"A demon?" Sybil squeaked, her gaze shooting back to Kenric's. "I thought they were the bad guys."

"Not all," Kenric answered. "His kind alone stood with us against the shadows. And now he is all that remains of his race."

"Adrian, that leaves you." She sought out the short-haired man. "So far we have a demon, a dragon, and a werewolf. What are you and what do you want to do to me?"

He moved closer. "What am I? A vampire. What do I want to do with you? All that I please." He let her see the bloodlust that gleamed in his deep brown eyes, and his smile took on a predatory edge.

She swallowed and felt her knees weaken. It was a good

thing Kadar was subtly supporting her. She didn't want to look like a fainting maiden. Or a snack.

"You didn't ask what I am." Ronan spoke again, drawing her attention.

She licked dry lips. "What are you?"

"Daoine sidhe."

The hard, masculine voice spoke with the music of Ireland, rolling out the syllables as *deena shee*. People of the mounds, Sybil thought with a shiver of wonder. The fae. That explained the height, the long, silver hair, the sharp, exotic features.

"Oh," she said.

"You should tell her the rest of it," Kadar prompted.

"What rest?" Sybil wasn't sure she wanted to know, but if there was more, she supposed she should hear it.

"It won't be only for five days and nights," Ronan answered. "Once ours, always ours."

"Always?" She stared at him in consternation, then found herself looking to Kenric again. "Like, any of you can have me any time you feel like it, for the rest of my life?"

"We won't take you unwillingly." Something like a wolfish smile touched his face. Probably remembering how willing she'd been with him already.

"Thoughtful of you." Her voice sounded as faint as she felt. "Can I point out there are five of you and one of me? It seems a tad inequitable. Am I supposed to be enough to go around, or will you be amusing yourselves with me along with your other lovers?"

"We will have other lovers." Kenric answered without hesitation.

Was that good or bad? Sybil tried to sort it out. On the plus side, she wouldn't be expected to satisfy all of them by herself indefinitely. On the negative side, what if she didn't like it with one of them? The rest of her life was a long time to have to stand ready to sleep with a man she might not like.

"Do you honestly think any of Inanna's chosen wouldn't know how to give pleasure as well as take it?" Kadar asked, openly amused by her thoughts.

"That mind-reading trick is getting really old," Sybil grumbled without heat. "Okay, wise guy, answer this one. Suppose I fall in love someday? Is my Mr. Right supposed to understand when I go off to screw you all periodically?"

"Yes."

"Yes?" She twisted around to gape at him in disbelief.

"Yes. Your bond to us predates any future commitment. He will have to understand that."

"That's going to really cut down on my dating pool."

"As opposed to the wide array of options currently open to you?" Kadar raised a sarcastic brow.

Sybil winced. "Point."

He caught her hand, turned it over and nibbled at her palm.

The fact that she enjoyed it only increased her apprehension. "Besides, once marked you can only be mate to one of us."

All the air left her lungs and her head went light. "Excuse me?"

"Any of us can claim you as mate," the dragon said.

She swallowed around the hard knot in her throat. "I see. And if that happens, does that mean I'm no longer expected to sleep with the others?"

"No. It means you'll be wife to one and a sort of junior wife to the rest." Kadar flicked his tongue over the pulse point at her inner wrist and laughed when she yanked her hand away.

"Do you still accept?" Kenric asked from behind her.

Sybil turned to face him. She met his golden gaze without flinching. "As our dragon friend so charmingly reminded me, I don't have a lot of choices here."

Especially after asking the goddess for help. Refusing the form that help took struck her as a greater risk. Sex really wasn't the worst thing that could happen to her. Although it was hard to look at the five of them and remember that. Did they have to look so intimidating?

"Is that a yes?" Kenric prompted.

Sybil searched his features for any hint that would clue her in to his feelings about the deal and found none. Did he want her to say yes? Either way, it was the only answer she could give. "Yes. I still accept."

"She was ready to accept you at the oasis," Kadar said.

"A gentleman would keep his mouth shut," Sybil said in a voice like sugar laced with arsenic.

"I'm no gentleman."

That went for all of them, Sybil felt sure. These weren't civilized men. If she was honest with herself, that held a certain appeal. Sex with them would be primal and raw. She didn't see any of them rolling over to fall asleep five minutes after getting started. Then again, holding their undivided attention had a downside. Was she really up to the task?

Heat seared her skin and that answered her question. She'd better be. The alternative was . . . bad. And not just for her. She had a responsibility to reverse the harm she'd unwittingly done, to turn back the chain of events she'd set in motion by finding that book.

"Do I start with you?" Sybil asked Kenric.

"Yes."

She nodded, trying to at least appear brave. "So, how do we do this?"

He reached out to her, fingered the fabric of her shirt. "First, you run."

"From you?"

"Later, yes. For now, from them." He made a gesture to her left. Sybil followed it with her eyes and felt her knees turn to water at the sight of a cluster of dark-winged things swooping down out of the night.

"Oh, shit," she whispered.

"Run," Kadar repeated Kenric's command. "Go here."

Her vision blurred as an image formed in her mind. An underground cave system. An entrance. A path, that way. "Got it."

Her feet took off without conscious direction, pounding against the ground in tandem with her pounding heart. Sheer terror gave her speed, but sustaining it made her muscles and lungs burn with effort. By the time she spotted the rocky hillside entrance that matched the picture in her head, her breath came in gasping gulps that would have drowned out the sounds of pursuit behind her. That thought made her look over her shoulder, and she tripped, half-falling into the cavern.

Behind her, a dragon swooped and a wolf leaped. A silver-haired form moved faster than her eye could follow, sword flashing. She couldn't see Adrian or Abaran in the melee, and found herself straining until she caught sight of each of them.

Sybil stumbled back deeper into the shelter Kadar had sent her to, her heart in her throat. Fear shot through her, not just for herself and for what might happen if the uncontrolled power inside her fell into the wrong hands, but for what might happen to the five strangers who intended to be her lovers and now fought to protect her.

five

Sybil cursed her uselessness as she searched the cavern for something she could use as a weapon if any of the creatures broke through and found her. Not trained as a fighter, not trained as a witch. Just a massive liability.

Not for long, she vowed, and contemplated the stalactites overhead. They glittered like ice, narrowing to sharp-looking points at the ends. Icicles made from limestone. Could she break one off to use as a sort of knife? Of course, she'd have to find a way to reach one first.

"Maybe you could just make a bomb out of lipstick and tissue, Ms. MacGyver," she said out loud. Her voice echoed off walls that glittered with phosphorescence and unknown minerals. A now-familiar burning itch ate at her hands, and Sybil looked down at them with narrowed eyes. If only all that power was good for something.

Of course, it was demon power and chaos demon power at that. Inherently unstable.

Sybil hovered between the battle outside and the possibility of getting hopelessly lost inside. The need to know what was happening won. She compromised by staying in the cavern's opening, a position that gave her shelter and a clear view.

Dark-winged creatures filled the air like stormclouds. Kadar stood out in vivid relief, his metallic hide flashing bright. His tail swept a patch of air clear, and à burst of flame from his open mouth cleared a much larger space. Dark bodies rained down and lay still.

Don't piss off the dragon. He breathes napalm.

Ronan and Adrian fought with swords, cutting down swathes of winged intruders as they moved like mad threshers bent on a bloody harvest. The agile form of a wolf leaped in and out of sight, fangs and claws tearing his enemies apart. Abaran swooped above them, driving the dark creatures within reach of the ground fighters and gutting more with some weapon that looked like a three-pronged spear.

When the invaders attempted a retreat, the five fanned out

to form a ring. There was a searing explosion of light. When Sybil's vision cleared, only the five guardians remained.

She wasted no time getting back out into the open. The giant black wolf came to meet her. The memory of Kenric in battle made her hesitate halfway. He hadn't meant it literally when he'd said she should run from him later. Had he?

The wolf backed up a few steps. Sybil took a cautious step forward. Then another. When it didn't leap at her, she relaxed a little of the tension that held her taut.

"Bad guys all gone?" Her voice squeaked a little, and Sybil winced at the sound.

The wolf looked at her as if she was an idiot for asking the obvious.

"Right." She cleared her throat. "So, um, what now?"

The wolf crouched down and stared at her. The attentive, alert gaze and the readiness in the pose alarmed her all over again. He wanted to play chase? After he'd fought off alien beings from the twilight zone?

A low sound rumbled in the wolf's chest. It sounded like the word run. Her pulse skipped and adrenaline flooded her system all over again.

Wolves liked to hunt. Now apparently he wanted to hunt her. Werewolf foreplay? Or was the animal in him looking for new prey?

For the second time that day, Sybil bolted. Kenric took off behind her. They both knew she couldn't outrun him, but when he didn't bring her down in the first few yards, determination kept her going. The wolf at her heels could catch her without even trying, but that didn't mean she wasn't going to put in an effort.

After a while, the rhythm of running became a soothing candence while a sense of inevitability built. Kenric would put an end to this chase sooner or later. He'd catch her. And then what? A kaleidoscope of sexual possibilities spun through her head.

As the distance grew, Sybil realized running was hard work. The strain on joints and ligaments, the jarring from a hard-packed, uneven surface, the ragged panting that passed for a full breath. She didn't have to look behind her to know that Kenric wasn't even starting to tire. Dammit. When she felt the pull of a stitch in her side, she gave up and collapsed onto the ground.

"Okay," she gasped out when she could spare enough air to feed her voice. "I get it. You're my new drill sergeant, and I'm the most pathetic excuse for a new recruit you've ever seen. You're going to whip me into shape."

"Something like that." Kenric's voice didn't sound strained at all, as if he'd just been out for a casual stroll. He'd shifted back to human form stood over her, naked, with his hands on his hips. His golden eyes burned with heated intent.

He looked like a predator ready to enjoy the prize he'd won. Sybil forgot to take in air.

"Breathe," Kenric told her.

Right. She tried to take deeper breaths and hold them in a little longer. The stitch in her side had eased as soon as she stopped running.

"Better."

Sybil made a face. "Glad you approve." Then she blurted out, "Are you glad I said yes to the deal?"

His jaw tightened. "Are you asking if I want you?"

She made a gesture with her hand. "I'm clarifying. We had a moment there, at the oasis."

"You had a need. I had a responsibility."

She gave him a disbelieving stare. "You had a hard-on."

Kenric's eyes narrowed and a series of little changes in his body language said *stop*. She ignored the warning. "Look, however you want to explain it, it happened. Now I'm going to be sleeping with you and four of your friends."

"We are representatives of a sex goddess," Kenric pointed out. "It doesn't make for a lot of taboos."

"And polyamory isn't unusual for witches."

"So there's no problem."

She was up to her neck in problems. "Fine." Sybil went back to focusing on her breathing.

"Get up."

"I am not running another step."

"Get up."

Sybil heaved a sigh and lumbered upright. "Don't look at me like that," she muttered. "I work in an office. There's not a lot of physical training involved." And she'd overdone it, showing off for him like an idiot.

"Walk."

"Sadist."

"Walk," Kenric repeated in a level voice. "Otherwise your muscles will tighten up and you'll hurt twice as much tomorrow. Walk it out now. You're going to need to be in top form to drive back what's after you."

"Good point." She took a tentative first step and kept going even though her feet throbbed from the unaccustomed pounding she'd put them through.

"Back that way."

"Right." Sybil turned around and began to walk, trying not to limp.

Kenric fell into step beside her. "You're limping."

She gritted her teeth. Like she needed a reminder that her physical condition wasn't a match for his. "I know."

They walked together in silence. Finally he said, "I want you."

She almost tripped over her own feet at the abrupt declaration. Kenric steadied her. She let him, feeling slightly stunned. The small contact carried a sexual charge she felt all the way to her toes.

He didn't speak again until they reached the cavern's entrance. He stopped and gestured for her to go first. "Inside."

Sybil went back into the cavern that provided its own soft light. He followed, then touched her waist to direct her.

"There's a heated mineral pool past the second cave," Kenric said.

"There's a reason to keep walking."

The last few yards passed in silence. She saw the steam rising from the pool before she saw the water, and stopped to take off her shoes and socks. Kenric went ahead of her and sank up to his shoulders.

She undid her pants and stripped them off, underwear included. Hanging onto them seemed pointless when he'd already seen what was underneath. Her shirt and bra went next. Then she followed Kenric into the pool. Blissful heat encased her. Bouyant water supported her. She let out a groan of pleasure, surrendering to the experience.

"Here."

Kenric reached for her, and Sybil obligingly swam toward him. He pulled her sideways into his lap and propped her head on his chest.

"Thanks." She relaxed into his hold, trusting him to keep her from drowning if she passed out. His hands moved over her arm and back, a soothing touch.

When he cupped her chin and raised it, the sight of his head bending to hers seemed the most natural thing in the world. She watched through half-closed eyes as he moved closer, then closed them completely as his mouth covered hers.

Warm, firm lips coaxed hers to soften and cling, then part. She felt the tip of his tongue probe at the small opening she'd made, tasting, tempting. She opened wider, giving in to temptation, offering him more. The kiss deepened, becoming an exploration of tongues as well as lips, a slow exchange that heated by degrees until she moved against him in restless need for more.

Hands reached out, gripped, stroked, discovering line and form and texture. His unerringly searched out points that made her shiver with sensation. Hers glided along hard muscle, the freedom to touch a pleasure and a reward in itself.

Languor spread through her body, made her relax further, molding herself to him. His touch grew harder, fingertips digging into muscle and then releasing, a sensual massage that drove her to turn in his lap until she straddled his thighs in an effort to get closer.

Her breasts felt tight and aching, nipples swollen and pouting for attention. She arched her back to press them harder against the wall of his chest. His hands moved down her spine, then lower until he cupped her hips, fingers splayed along the soft flesh of her ass. He drew her more fully into his embrace, until her mound met his groin and her belly molded against the tumescent heat of his cock. She wanted that pressure lower, and moved her hips in silent request. His hands tightened, holding her still.

The kiss went on and on, the slide of his tongue against hers, the hungry demand of his lips a seduction in itself. When he raised his head to leave a gap between them, her lips felt bereft and cold.

"Would you have let me take you at the oasis?"

The question broke through the sensual haze. "Mmm? Yes."

"Even though you knew I wasn't a man."

Sybil struggled to focus, heavy lids raising with an effort. "You may not be human, but you're a man."

"And you may not be werewolf, but you're female."

The statement seemed to hold some cryptic meaning for him, but deciphering it would take too much concentration. Sybil let it go and leaned up the tiny bit required to close the gap between them, to kiss him again and then again. The fact that he spent some time in animal form seemed irrelevant. What mattered was this, the rush of blood that beat inside her with increasing urgency, the sweet ache of need between her thighs.

Rising up to kiss him made her body ride higher against his. She felt her sex make contact with his turgid length, his shaft pressing her clitoris. It felt unimaginably good. She glided up and down, stroking herself over him as her tongue mated with his.

Kenric ended the kiss and tightened his grip on her, stilling her motion while holding her close. She breathed out a soft sigh and turned her cheek to rest against him, floating in a sensual dream as the heated water and heated male combined to soothe away the stresses of the day.

"Did anybody get hurt?" Sybil asked the question in a small voice. She'd been too far away to tell.

"No."

She exhaled relief. "What were those things?"

"Demons."

"Were they after me?"

"They seek the book. The gate's opened, and the spell that did it left a clear signature."

"Is it safe here?"

"As safe as anywhere. One of us will remain on guard at all times, and call in the others as needed until the gate is closed."

Sybil nodded. After a few minutes, she whispered, "I'm sorry."

"Sorry?"

"Sorry I found the damn thing. Sorry I picked it up. Sorry

I wanted so badly to claim my heritage as a witch that I let it get the better of my common sense. I should have put it back as soon as I saw what it was."

"Really? Did you know it was demonic power seeking an outlet?"

"Well, no. I thought it was just an ordinary book of shadows."

Kenric stroked an idle hand down her spine as he spoke. "Even if you had tried to put it back, it wouldn't have let you. You didn't find it by chance. It revealed itself to you."

She grimaced. "What, I fit its victim profile?"

"Something like that."

So she'd been doomed from the moment she'd given in to impulse and pulled off to browse the estate sale. "I should have kept driving."

"Since you can't go back in time and change a past mistake, you'll have to live with it."

The withdrawal in Kenric's tone washed through her like cold water. He set her aside and gestured toward the edge of the pool. "You've soaked long enough. Come."

The moment was definitely over. Sybil nodded and climbed out, then stood dripping in the cool air. "Now what?"

"Follow."

She blew out a breath, dislodging the curl over her eye, and made her way after Kenric, staying close behind him. When she stepped on something soft, she started and looked down. "Is that moss?"

"Keep walking."

They were in a corridor, she saw, and the walls were definitely covered with more than minerals and phosphorescence now. Green vines. Flowers. The corridor widened and led into an enormous open . . . meadow?

Sybil looked around in wonder and saw twin moons high overhead, trees in the distance, grass and more flowers under her feet.

"Daoine sidhe," she murmured. There were stories about the fairy mounds, the worlds underground with strange suns and moons, where time was measured differently. "Did Ronan make this?"

"Yes. Long ago. Xanadu is his creation and our home."

"Wow." The word was inadequate, but nothing else came to mind. Moonlight washed the meadow in a silvery glow, making dew sparkle on petals and leaves as if they were outlined in diamonds.

The residual heat from the water and exertion kept her from getting chilled, but Sybil knew it wouldn't last. So she didn't protest when Kenric went on instead of lingering. The path from the meadow led to a stone den with engraved figures she didn't recognize around the opening. Then they were inside, and Sybil found herself toeing a pile of furs.

"Decadent."

"Practical." Kenric shrugged and sank down, then held out a hand to her. Sybil took it and joined him. The fur felt cool to the touch, soft and silky, a deep plush that gave beneath her and soothed her bare skin.

She glanced around at the enclosed space. Cozy, if you liked the stone age look. Stone and fur, with a magical meadow to another world just outside.

"You run like wounded prey," Kenric informed her.

"Ah, the pillow talk begins." She flopped onto her back and squirmed into a comfortable position. "You, on the other hand, run like a predator. Oh, wait, that's because you are."

"I know how to run as a man, too."

"I'll get better." She rolled onto her stomach and closed her eyes in sheer bliss as softness touched her everywhere.

"You don't know the most elemental magic," he went on, apparently determined to list all her faults.

"Yes, and you know why, so I don't think you should blame me for it." Sybil levered herself up to scowl at Kenric. "I was trying to learn. I wanted to reach my potential. That's how I ended up here."

"Do you really want to reach your potential?" Disconcerting golden eyes stared into hers.

"Yes."

"Then we should begin."

Sybil licked dry lips. "I'm ready."

"Not yet, but you will be." His voice sounded like a dark promise. He moved closer and put a hand between her shoulder blades to press her down. She let him, relaxing back into the softness that cradled her. His hand moved lower, stroked over the curves of her butt, then nudged her thighs apart until his fingertips brushed her sex.

He teased the soft curls between her legs, caressed her labia, subtly increasing pressure until she felt her flesh softening and giving way. One fingertip probed deeper and she let out a soft breath at the intimate exploration.

He pushed forward, slowly working his way in, withdrew, stroked inside her again. Sybil felt her inner muscles tightening around his digit in an involuntary response.

"Like that, do you, witch?" Kenric slid his finger out of her sheath, added a second, and tested her reaction as he probed her slick tissues. She made a soft moan of an answer and arched her back, trying to take him deeper. The extra width when she wasn't quite ready was almost but not quite too much, and it made her want more.

The third finger pressed inside, stroked, teased, withdrew, and slid further, seeking her clit. When it made contact, the stimulation made her pelvis rock.

"Closer," Kenric murmured. He toyed with her, first stroking the delicate bundle of nerves, then slowly working his third finger all the way inside her tight sex again.

She'd been close at the pool, and he'd stopped her, but Sybil didn't complain. Instead, she moved her thighs wider apart, raised her buttocks, and gave herself over to the sensation of being intimately touched and pleasured by a man's hand without any other part of their bodies meeting.

He stroked inside her, withdrew to caress and stroke her clit, pressing his palm over her sex, then drawing a fingertip along her open folds before abruptly plunging two fingers deep.

The rhythm varied, shifting before she could follow it, leaving her to tremble in anticipation. It felt so good. It wasn't enough. That gliding caress over her swollen clit sent sensation jolting through her. The penetration of his fingers built a frustrated need for more. He never touched her deeply enough, long enough. Then he withdrew completely, robbing her of all touch.

"On your knees."

She rose up onto hands and knees without thinking, and then he was behind her, between her open legs, and she felt the head of his cock against her slick folds. He was going to take her. Now. Like this. Anticipation made her breath catch. Magic gathered and pulsed in the air.

He felt larger than she'd expected, hard and hot and male. His hands gripped her hips and then he was pushing into her

as she gave way to the intimate pressure, softened tissues parting and opening to accept him. He pushed forward steadily
until he was buried in her to the hilt, making her stretch to
take all of him. She felt almost unbearably full. The unaccustomed depth and width of his penetration had her squirming
while he held still as she attempted to accommodate all of him.

"Maybe you should pull out and try again," Sybil suggested, panting a little. "I think we need a different position."

"Too late." He swelled inside her and she gasped at the
sensation. He was even deeper inside her and he hadn't moved.

"What do you mean, too late?" She turned to look at him
over her shoulder. His jaw was set, his face hard, eyes glitter-
ing in the dim light.

"I mean too late. I can't withdraw until I've spent myself
inside you."

She sucked in a breath. "What?"

"It's a sex trait of wolves. A knot forms during intercourse
to lock a pair together and doesn't release until after ejacula-
tion."

That was Mother Nature for you, thought Sybil. Ruthlessly
practical when it came to ensuring continuation of the species.
"Nice time to mention it."

"It shouldn't have happened with a human," Kenric ground
out. "You're not a wolf. I would have mentioned it if I'd thought
it would come up."

So why had it? There was an unanswerable question. Instead of trying, Sybil experimented with shifting her position until she found a more comfortable angle by lowering her arms and torso. That left her tightened nipples brushing the fur beneath her. The extra stimulation became a constant caress as Kenric began to move inside her, making her body rock forward, then back with his thrusts.

She focused on opening herself to him, surrendering to the tight fit of his flesh in hers and the gathering power that flowed back and forth between them, building with each movement. He pressed so deep it made her breath catch, the friction of his shaft moving inside her sheath growing more pleasurable as additional lubrication eased his entry.

He moved again, and it abruptly became a lot more pleasurable. Then ecstatic.

"Kenric," she moaned. "Yes. Oh, please, yes."

As if her words were the signal he'd been waiting for, he began to pump his hips into her, driving his cock as far as he could, as far as she could take it, while she strained to take more.

six

Sybil's world narrowed to the bed of furs beneath her, the male body behind hers, locked with hers, the thick shaft that rode endlessly into her. The first time she came, she writhed and bucked and panted while he continued to thrust in a steady rhythm. The second time, it took longer to build and lasted longer, a seemingly endless wave of pleasure and magic so intense she wasn't sure she could endure it. She ground herself against his groin, moaning and spasming.

When it finally ended, it started all over again. Kenric's pace increased, demanding more of her, taking her harder, deeper, until she felt the next peak forming. She closed her eyes and braced for the intensity of it. The hard male cock inside her throbbed and jerked, a precursor of his own release, and Sybil realized this one they'd share. Tiny ripples of ecstasy made her inner muscles grip his shaft and cling. A low growl came from behind her, sending a shiver of danger down her spine that heightened her awareness of him.

Not safe, she thought, arching her back to offer more of herself to him. This was not safe. She didn't care. She wanted this. She wanted him. She forgot everything but the two of them, the demands of his cock and her acquiescence, following the pace he set, a willing participant as he led her past the point of no return. She felt him pulse inside her, felt an answering pulse in her womb, and then the rhythm became a driving frenzy as he began to spill hot liquid into her core.

He fucked her almost furiously, inciting an equally wild response as the violence of their mutual release surged through them and power grounded itself in her flesh. The shock of the burning sensation on her breast made her cry out. Heat scored her skin while the last of her orgasm wrung her. Kenric continued to slam into her as if he wanted to drive his seed further in. Her muscles went slack and she crumpled under him, spent. He came to rest deep inside her.

"Witch?"

"It worked," Sybil mumbled. "I felt it burn into me. Like a brand."

He turned them both on their sides so they lay spooned, flesh still locked together. His hand explored her breast with a gentle touch. She let out a huff of breath at the electric discharge when his fingertip grazed the two points of a partial star. Like the mark reacted to the one who'd given it.

"Branded you," Kenric murmured.

She felt his cock twitch inside her and wondered if the satisfaction in his tone was her imagination. She felt branded by him, and not just where it showed. She'd had sex before. She'd never felt so utterly possessed in the act. Claimed.

"Thought that was the idea," Sybil said, trying for a light tone.

"It is." He sent his hand lower, closed his thumb and forefinger over her distended nipple. The pressure made her womb clench. He felt it and sent his cock deeper into her in response.

"So we're done?" She didn't want to be done. After the way he'd taken her, she might never want to be done.

"No." He released her nipple and reached down to cup his hand above her mound, his fingertips brushing the place where their bodies joined. "After a day and a night we'll be done." He searched out her clit, stroked it. "Until then, your body is mine to use, and I intend to use it hard."

She sucked in a breath at the exquisite sensations he aroused and the heated intent in his voice.

"Use me," she invited.

"Do you think you can stand?"

Sybil blinked. "Uh, yes. Why?"

Kenric pulled out of her, the suddenness of it leaving her empty and stunned. "I want you bent over that wall." He indicated a ledge on the far side of the small room.

Sybil managed to get her feet under herself and stood. Then she made her way to the spot he'd chosen. The rock formed a natural shelf at a convenient height. If she stood with her legs shoulder width apart and bent forward from the waist, it would support her fairly comfortably.

"Like this?" She asked the question over her shoulder, and drew in her breath sharply when she realized he was right behind her.

"Exactly like that."

Her eyes dropped to his midsection. His cock jutted toward her, heavily engorged, thick and ready. Her sex clenched in greedy anticipation.

"Bend lower," Kenric instructed. She wiggled her feet a little further apart and leaned into position. "Lower. Arch your back until I can see your pink pussy."

The graphic words made her brows rise. They also made her hot. She displayed herself to him and felt her breath come faster as he stood in silence behind her, knowing where his eyes were resting.

"Is this what I'm offered?" She felt his finger push into her slick flesh.

"Yes." Her voice was as uneven as her breathing.

"Soft and ready." He sent a second finger to join the first, twisting them inside her. Then he withdrew. She felt him guide the head of his cock to her opening, aligning himself, preparing to thrust deep. She waited, anticipation coiling tight as the seconds dragged out. Then he plunged into her, hard and fast. The fit was no less snug the second time, but her body had had a chance to become accustomed to his and she was able to take him without a slow entry.

"I won't take it easy on you this time," she heard him say. Her pulse leaped in response.

Kenric looked at the narrow back below him, the rounded hips and the soft swells of bare buttocks that cushioned his thrusts. The witch looked far too fragile, slender and fine-boned, pale as porcelain. She couldn't fight, she couldn't run, and yet the power to undo worlds lay within her. He looked higher, taking in the vulnerable curve of her neck that he longed to rake with his teeth and the tousled curls that tempted his fingers unreasonably.

Well, why not? She was his. He suited action to impulse, threading one hand into her hair and making a fist, not quite pulling at the roots but getting her attention. He bent over her, covering the column of her spine with his torso, setting the edge of his teeth against that sensitive skin, nipping sharply.

She responded with an inarticulate groan, arching under him, the tightening clasp of her flesh around his shaft a clear sign that his rough play excited her.

Not too rough, though. He gauged her capacity and worked her body with measured skill. She could take so much pressure here, find just that much pleasurable there before it crossed a line. At least one of their number would take her across those lines. Knowing that drove him to push her to the limit. By the end of her time with him, she would learn to go further. It might prepare her for the unique pleasure she'd find in Ronan's punishment.

"Witch," he muttered in a voice thick with lust and old anger at her kind. He didn't want to want her. Why did his flesh form the knot inside her, as if mating?

"Wolf," she countered, panting. "Kiss me."

Kiss her. He'd made that mistake at the pool, claiming her mouth. She'd turned the tables and nearly seduced him. The memory of her body gliding along his, her face soft and flushed and dreamy, made his cock harden further.

Witches were dangerous. He couldn't forget that no matter how much his body craved more of hers. But he'd keep her at a safe distance while taking what she offered so willingly.

"Kenric," Sybil sighed, the silky clasp of her sheath tightening around his invading cock. The sound of his name, spoken in her passion-drugged voice, pleased him. Their position pleased him even more. She was submissive to him, acknowledging his superior strength. Knot or no knot, he was in control. He would make her come when he chose, as often as he chose.

She rocked her hips to welcome his strokes, gripped him with rippling inner muscles that told him how close she was to going over the edge again. He growled against the base of her neck, nipping down firmly on her skin but taking care not to break the surface, and took her with measured force.

When he'd pushed her to come for him twice, he raised her torso up by tugging at her scalp until she followed his direction. That allowed his hands ready access to the naked curves of her breasts.

"Small," he said, knowing the word would goad her as he sent his thumbs over the stiff points of her nipples.

She didn't answer, rolling her head back against the curve of his shoulder, baring her throat in an unconsciously submissive posture that made his cock jerk in eagerness. Her lids were lowered, so thin they seemed almost translucent, the brown silk of her lashes laying against her pale skin.

"Is this all you have to offer?" He palmed her breasts roughly, squeezed with deliberate crudity as if testing her for ripeness and finding her lacking.

That scored more of a reaction than he expected. He felt heat flash just below the surface of her skin an instant before her eyes flew open, lips parting in a gasp as she went rigid. She burned in his hands, writhing as she fought to control the demonic power her flesh seemed too fragile to contain.

"I have you," he ground out, holding her fast.

Her breath came faster, nearly a sob, but she nodded and pressed closer to him.

"Think of me. Only me," he ordered. He ran his hands over her breasts, down her belly, teased the silky curls at the apex of her thighs, and then sought out the sensitive bud of flesh that hid beneath its protective hood. She needed to focus and release the heat inside her. "Open your legs wider."

She did, moving restlessly as waves of fever rose from her bare skin. He scored the curve of her neck with the edge of his teeth, then traced the line with his tongue. Then he pushed her down again until her breasts lay against cool rock and her butt rose up, deepening the angle of his penetration.

He took her with animalistic hunger, knew she'd locked onto the escape valve he provided when her skin paled again. She responded to the driving force of his cock tunneling into her tight flesh with eager welcome, crying out as his head found the opening to her womb, squirming as her body tightened in building pleasure.

He felt his balls contract, took her harder, faster, and gave himself up to the primitive satisfaction of spending himself in her depths.

Afterward, he felt the knot release and withdrew. She didn't move, didn't make a sound. Kenric slapped her bare ass with an open palm.

"Get up."

"Can't."

"No stamina."

"Kids today." Her lips curved in a satisfied half-smile, agreeing with him while she mocked him.

"Get up." He ran his palm over the inviting curve of her butt. "Unless you want me to use this."

She stirred and then stilled. "Can't stop you."

She really couldn't move? He worked his hands under her until he could lift her upright. "Lazy witch."

"If you want me to have more energy in bed, don't make me race you first." She ended the suggestion with a yawn.

Kenric bent and put his shoulder into her midsection, draping her over his torso with her bare ass pointed skyward. She sagged bonelessly in his hold, proof of either utter exhaustion or deep trust. The prospect of either made him frown.

He deposited her into the nest of furs that made up his bed with a lack of ceremony that should have roused her to complain. Instead, she made a contented sound and curled into a ball. Her breathing deepened almost instantly.

Kenric prodded her side with his foot. "Did I give you permission to sleep?"

She struggled to raise her lids and made it halfway. "Don't make me want to hit you. It'll just frustrate me because I don't have the energy after that."

He joined her, settled himself on his back, and then pulled her slender body to rest atop his. His arms secured her in position. "Sleep there."

"Um," she agreed, snuggling close as if she never wanted to be anywhere else.

Her curls tickled his chin. The silken expanse of her skin felt exotic against his, the softness of her breasts a reminder of her femininity. The distinctive scent of woman filled his nostrils, mingled with the sharp tang of magic and the subtle fragrance of herbs. *Witch.*

He drew a fur over them, tucking it around her to ward off any possibility of a chill. Now that the dangerous surge of heat had left her, her body felt too cool.

She rubbed her cheek against his chest. "Kenric," she murmured.

He ran an idle hand over her curls in response. She breathed out and he felt her body go limp as sleep took her. His hand remained where it was, cupping the back of her head.

He was still awake, listening to the rhythm of her breathing, when it hitched, then sped up. Heat flared from her skin.

"Witch," Kenric said gruffly, weaving his fingers into her hair to tug at her scalp. She didn't wake. Her skin felt scalding against his. "Sybil." He said her name louder. She stirred, made a soft sound of distress, but slept on.

The heat intensified. How broad a temperature range could the human frame endure? Kenric thought it was a narrow difference. Was the demonic power inside her trying to get free by destroying its prison of flesh?

"Sybil." He said it in a tone of harsh command. Her lashes fluttered weakly. "Wake. Fight."

Her head moved, and he saw her bite down on her lower lip as if resisting the compulsion to give voice to a spell. Was she losing the inner battle? Sudden fear for her made him move fast. He pulled her body up his, felt her thighs fall to either side of his hips, drew her back down until his cock aligned with her opening. Then he held her firmly in place while he thrust up, impaling her with his rigid shaft.

She curled into him, clung, and rocked with the rhythm he established. Taking him, giving herself, channeling the roiling power inside her that strove to find expression into motion. She rode him to an urgent climax, then transitioned to a slower, steady pace he found exquisite. Her buttocks flexed under his hands as her pelvis tilted to take him deep into her welcoming core, angled back as he partially withdrew, tilted again to maximize penetration.

He rubbed his chin against the top of her head, dug his fingers into the soft, giving flesh of her ass, pulled her hips into his as he surged inside her slick, silken sheath. He let one hand move lower, stroking her buttocks, tracing the valley between, searching out the puckered opening there. He stroked the sensitive region with fingertips. She squirmed in response, wiggling her ass as he caressed her anus.

"You like having your pussy full of thick, hard cock," he murmured. "How do you like taking one here?"

She stilled. "I don't know. I've never tried it."

Kenric pressed the pad of his fingertip against her tight opening. "How does that feel?"

"Good." The surprised arousal in her voice made him want to smile.

At least one other of their number would enter her there while two or more were sharing her. It would be easier for her if he began to prepare her now.

As if she'd picked up Kadar's trick for mind-reading, she asked, "Will any of the others want that?"

"Yes."

She swallowed. "Oh." She raised her head to look at him, her blue eyes wide and serious. "I don't know about the rest, but I got a good look at Kadar's equipment. I'm not sure that's going to work."

He imagined her on her knees, ass upturned, cheeks parted,

rosy aperture stretching as the shaft of a penis pushed inside. Imagined himself filling her sex, feeling her wrapped even more tightly around his cock as she was stretched to the limit to accommodate two lovers. Being shared so intimately would take her to new heights. If he thought she'd be ready to accept it now, he would invite another to join them. "It's easier with practice."

Sybil regarded him in silence, then stretched her torso along his again. "I like the way your hand feels there."

Kenric continued to push lightly against the tight opening with the pad of his finger as he thrust into her sheath. Gradually he increased the pressure until she'd taken the tip of his finger. Then he began to work her delicate tissues with tiny, shallow movements. He heard her breathing quicken, felt her sex grow slicker, then felt the ripple of her inner muscles gripping his shaft tighter that signaled approaching orgasm.

His own wasn't far off. He thrust harder between her legs. His finger drove deeper into her ass. She began to moan and make urgent, restless movements that made him ache to come inside her. Knowing she could take more at the edge of release, he increased the speed and pressure of his finger. The way she welcomed the twin invasion of his hand and cock brought him abruptly to the brink. He began to spill himself into her tight, welcoming heat while she cried out and came with him.

Afterward, she sprawled on his chest, panting. He liked the

fact that the intensity of her response left her spent. Liked having her body still twice penetrated by his. Most of all, he found a perverse pleasure in knowing that for the moment she was his alone.

sybil woke up alone. She rolled over, grimaced as muscles lodged loud complaints, and sat up. Sitting up felt a little awkward. She remembered Kenric's finger thrusting in and out of her anus while she rode him, and blushed. That had been interesting, not unpleasant, and if it made it a little hard to sit down the next day, it meant she needed a lot more practice. Kenric had been clear about what the others would expect of her.

She swallowed hard, thinking about that. Her twenty-four hours wasn't up yet, but it had to be day now. Tonight, she'd be in another man's bed. Or cave. Or cage. Goddess only knew what waited for her. In the meantime, she was the sexual property of a wolf who might appear, hungry for more, at any moment.

That thought galvanized her to action. She got to her feet and made her way out. The sight of the meadow under a distant sun seemed no less mysterious than the light of twin moons. The colors looked more vivid, richer, the textures more distinct by day. The blossoms and vines weren't like any she'd ever seen before. In the distance, she thought she heard the sound of a river and it didn't seem impossible that it emptied into an otherwordly sea.

She walked barefoot through velvet grass and spongy moss until her soles gripped cool stone again. The pool wasn't hard to find, now that she knew where to look. The dim light of the cavern was the same by day or night, making it impossible to measure time. For that matter, the position of the sun in the meadow didn't necessarily correspond to the one outside. She might have hours remaining to dally with a wolf in man form. Or not.

Sybil ducked under the water, washed herself as well as she could with her hands, then swam around to stretch stiff muscles.

"Good," Kenric said, startling her. "Swimming is excellent conditioning."

She stood up, which put the water level just below her breasts. Her nipples tightened from the contrast between warm water and cool air. "Glad you approve."

"It's a beginning." He gestured for her to come closer. She did, wondering if he'd greet her with a kiss, throw her to the ground and thrust inside her with no preliminaries, or drag her out to make her run for him again while he critiqued her form.

All options seemed equally likely.

Instead, he surprised her with none of the above.

"It's time we began your training."

seven

My what?" Sybil stared at Kenric. Images of him in drill sergeant uniform filled her mind. "I was kidding about being a lousy new recruit you had to whip into shape."

"I wasn't." He made a come-here gesture.

She waded out, feeling the water resistance dragging at her muscles. "I don't think I'm in shape for this."

"You said you wanted to reach your potential." Kenric stepped back and watched her, his golden eyes unreadable.

"Me and my big mouth."

"Let's begin with what you know," Kenric went on as if she hadn't spoken.

"I know theory. It's practical application I'm short on. I was only taught the most rudimentary spells. Things like consecrating objects, cleansing, casting circles." And now she was a living repository for a whole catalog of spells she didn't dare use. Irony.

"Spells exist to raise power and focus it. Raising power you do without effort. Now you will to learn to draw it as you will and focus it to your intent."

"And the mark helps with this?" Sybil asked, feeling hopeful.

"It helps you gain control, so you direct the power rather than being directed by it."

She hummed the *Mission Impossible* theme as he proceeded to drill her on focusing and aiming magical energy.

"Use the mark," he said in an even, patient tone, adjusting her stance and the position of her hands. He stood just behind her, his touch light and impersonal. "Draw power."

She tried to will that surge of heat to the surface. The effort made her tremble.

"Again. Don't strain."

Sybil blew the lock of hair out of her eyes, let her arms fall to her sides, and swung them to loosen up. Then she brought her hands back up to chest height, palms out, concentrating.

Nothing. No prickling or burning. "I think my batteries are dead."

"Again," Kenric repeated.

She sighed. "When I called you a drill sergeant, I had no idea how true that was." She focused, struggling to bring a rush of power to the surface. Or even a tiny flicker. Her hands dropped. "It's no use. I can't make it happen. It always happens involuntarily."

"Involuntary response can be trained to conscious control." His tone remained bland and unreadable as he moved around to face her. "Once more."

She raised her hands again and imagined throttling him. A stinging sensation made her rub her palms together, and a spark leapt between her hands. "Oh." Her eyes went wide.

"As I told you."

"Nobody likes a man who says I told you so," Sybil muttered. But she kept on concentrating, encouraged by that tiny proof, until at last Kenric told her to stop.

"Enough."

She nodded, her arms trembling with exertion. Sweat made tendrils of hair cling to the back of her neck. "I think I need another bath."

"I don't mind a body warm from exercise." He moved close, bent his head toward a bare breast, and laved her nipple. The slide of his tongue against her flesh seduced her. Sybil felt her peaks grow taut at his attention. He drew her aureole fully into his mouth, suckled hard, released it and then traced a fingertip around the dampened pink bud.

"Really," Sybil managed to say.

For an answer, he gave her other breast the same treatment. She glanced down and saw that his penis was erect and engorged. Kenric saw her look and something flickered in the depths of his golden eyes.

"Your turn." He put his hands on her shoulders and urged her to kneel. Then he fisted his hands in her short curls and guided her mouth to his shaft.

She kissed the length of him from the base of his balls up to the crown, then ran her tongue across the top, tasting salt and male musk. She opened to draw the head of his cock into her mouth and had to widen her jaw when he pushed forward, thrusting into her mouth. She wrapped her lips around his shaft and sucked as he moved back and forth, the slide of his flesh an exotic texture that teased her tongue. She laved the head, licked at his length as he fed himself into her mouth, and opened wider, angling her head to take him deeper.

"Will you swallow me if I spill myself on your tongue?" Kenric asked.

Sybil nodded and increased the suction she was giving him, suddenly hungry for the taste of him and the liquid proof that she could pleasure him.

"Perhaps later." He pulled himself out of her mouth. Sybil made a soft sound of protest, and buried her face against him, moving lower to run her tongue over the sensitive skin drawn tight over his balls. He lowered himself to his knees, facing her. "Lie back."

She did, feeling her nipples swelling and her sex clenching in anticipation. No matter how many times he touched her, it was never enough.

"Spread your thighs."

She slid her feet apart.

"Wider."

"Like this?" Sybil bent her knees and turned them out, opening herself to him.

"Like that." Kenric studied her for a moment, then brought his head down to claim first one nipple, then the other, suckling her until her womb clenched in response, raking the upper curves with his teeth, sliding up to lick the hollows of her collarbone. "Head back."

Sybil raised her chin and closed her eyes as she felt his mouth grazing the vulnerable curve of her exposed throat. Then he moved down and licked the seam of her sex. Once. Twice. The third time, his tongue circled her clit, licked it, before he drew his tongue lower and plunged it into her.

He suckled and tasted her sex until she was trembling and panting, her hips rocking in silent invitation. He raised his head and looked at her, sprawled in naked abandon, then cupped a hand between her thighs. His fingertips toyed with her slick flesh, caressing and probing lightly between her swollen labia, stroking her clit.

"Turn over."

Sybil rolled onto her stomach, sucking in a breath when he took her hips and pulled them up, adjusting her position so that she kneeled with her ass in the air, legs open, head resting on her hands.

He moved between her thighs, plunged two fingers into her slick heat, smoothed her own lubrication over the exposed rosette of her anus, and pushed first one, then the second digit inside.

She let out her breath in a rush and almost forgot to breathe in as he stretched her wider, making her burn for more. Two fingers were an almost uncomfortably tight fit, but at the same time the exotic sensation as he worked them in and out was a pleasure in itself. She made a low sound of encouragement and arched her lower back as he pushed in, stretched his fingers apart inside her, withdrew until she held only his fingertips.

Kenric cupped her sex with his free hand and plunged two more fingers into her slick sheath, opening her, stroking inside her, echoing his treatment of her anal passage. "Like that, witch?"

"Yes."

He withdrew his hands and then she felt him guiding his shaft close, the head of his cock nudging between her labia. Desire made her soft, slick, and welcoming, and he filled her unresisting flesh as she arched her lower back to take him deeper.

"DON'T go to sleep. I'm not finished with you, witch." The guttural growl made her smile as Sybil turned her face toward his. She floated in his arms while he washed her, using the water as an excuse to touch every part of her body.

"You might have finished me," she said. After her training session, he'd taken her from behind in a lengthy, thorough demonstration of his considerable stamina.

"You need building up if kneeling to receive my cock exhausted your endurance."

"You underestimate yourself." She gave him a lazy, satisfied smile.

"Pleased, are you?" Kenric kneaded the slight swells of her breasts as he spoke, making her smile widen.

"Uh-huh."

He played her sensitive nipples with expert skill, rousing her all over again. Sybil wrapped her legs around his waist, anchoring herself to him, feeling drunk with pleasure and unable to resist the need to get closer. He hooked his arms under hers and pulled her upright. Her nipples rubbed his chest, the intimate contact making her breasts ache for more.

"Witch."

"You say that like it's a bad thing." She wound her arms around his neck and kissed him, open-mouthed and eager, twining her tongue with his. He growled against her lips and devoured her, taking the opening she'd given him and using it to assert his dominance, while she willingly relinquished control.

When he broke the kiss, she felt dazed and breathless, lips swollen.

"I have no use for witches."

"Really?" She wiggled her belly against his tumescent penis. "Could have fooled me."

"No use, but one." Kenric put his hands on her waist, lifted her up until the head of his cock probed between her parted thighs.

"And they say romance is dead." Sybil grinned at him and then tucked her head under his chin as he pulled her body down until he was sheathed in her to the hilt. Her breath hitched as she felt the now-familiar swelling deep inside that indicated the knot was forming, locking their bodies together until release freed them.

"Do you want romance?" He gripped her hips with inexorable pressure, holding her fast, impaled. "Would you prefer sweet words from the man you spend tonight with? Or sweet satisfaction?"

Sybil felt a shiver run through her at the thought of the coming night. Whatever waited for her, it wasn't romance. "Stop talking," she whispered. She wanted to hold onto this moment. This man. The moment she went to her next lover, everything would shift.

"What about the night after? When the man I pass you to passes you on to the next and your body aches for release?" He growled the words in a darkly seductive voice, making her imagine the procession of lusty men taking her, one after another. Imagined the sensory overload of multiple hands on her body. Her inner muscles tightened and her breath quickened. Then a frission of alarm triggered a less welcome reaction.

She felt prickling heat sting her palms first, then spread up her arms. "Stop it."

"All five of us will have you," Kenric went on, relentlessly driving it home as he drove deeper into her. "One after another. Separately and together. Again and again."

The fantasy was undeniably erotic, but what would the reality be? His blunt words excited and disturbed her in equal measure. What if she couldn't handle it? The unstable emotions, combined with her intense response to Kenric's possession of her body, sent heat searing through her as power surged up and sought an outlet. Ghost flames burst from her arms.

"Burning for it, are you?" He tightened his grip on her and took her with furious force. "Burn for this. Burn for me, witch. Spread your legs wider while I use you hard."

Sybil struggled for control, opened herself further to accept the thick shaft he drove into her, and willed the flames away. She almost blinked in amazement when they banked, taking the scorching heat with them.

"That's it, witch." Kenric shifted, sliding one arm up her spine to fist his hand in her hair. He pulled her head back, covered her mouth with his. He kept on kissing her well after he'd emptied his balls into her womb.

Much later, Sybil stirred as she felt Kenric's hand stroke the bare curve of her ass.

"Again?" She asked, not certain if she wanted the answer to be yes. The more he had of her, the more she felt as if she was losing parts of herself to him. Parts she wasn't sure she'd take with her when she left him.

What if it was like that with all of them? What if they took her by turns until there was nothing left? She wasn't up to their level. They were supernatural studs. She was an incompetent witch who wore an A cup. They were into partner swapping, anal sex, BDSM, and who knew what else. She thought oral sex with a stranger was going over the edge of reason.

"No."

But he was still touching her, and she didn't move away. She couldn't bear to lose that small contact yet. Being with him had proven more intense and more intimate than she'd expected, and she wasn't ready to separate.

His hand traced up the line of her spine, back down to caress the beginning swell of her buttocks, then pushed into the crease formed by the insides of her thighs pressed together.

Sybil shifted her legs apart at his silent urging and he reached low between them to stroke her sex, petting and soothing as if to compensate for the animalistic way he'd claimed her in the pool.

"Turn over."

She rolled onto her back, legs slightly parted. He leaned up over her on one elbow as he ran a hand over her, tracing the hollows of her throat, the slopes of her breasts, the plane of her belly, the curve of her mound. His hand came to rest there, palm cupping her sex. He stroked her pubic curls and Sybil felt her throat tighten. She was glad when he didn't speak. That would mean he wouldn't expect her to, and she didn't trust her voice.

Even if she could speak, what could she say? "You knotted me, tell me what that means"? Or worse, "I think I might die if you don't touch me often enough for the rest of my life"?

He'd sounded like he was gargling gravel when she got him

to admit that he wanted her. There probably wasn't anything she could say that he'd welcome hearing right now.

Kenric gave her a final caress, rose to his feet, and extended his hand to help her up. He didn't keep her hand in his as they walked. Instead, he released her and took the lead, leaving her to follow behind him. She looked down at the mark on her skin. Four more nights, four more days, and the star would be complete.

Already she could see the plan working. She was gaining control. The partial mark she wore now had been enough to allow her to quiet the flames that erupted when Kenric goaded her. She would live, she would master the thing inside her, and close the damned gate. It was a fair trade.

The tightness in her throat constricted her breath. She didn't protest when Kenric led her deep into a dim, luminescent cavern and manacled her wrists and ankles to a large rock. The manacles pulled her arms up over her head, thrusting her naked breasts forward, and forced her legs wide apart, exposing her sex to full view of anyone. The position left her resting on her butt with her feet just off the ground, upright but angled back on the cold, rough stone.

"A gift to appease you, dragon," he called out.

She heard a scrape of talon on stone, saw a flicker of flame, and then the enormous beast padded toward her, tail flicking from side to side like a cat sighting prey and preparing to pounce.

"Not a virgin, I hope," the beast purred.

"Not between her thighs," Kenric said. "She's well able to take you."

"Is she?" The beast tilted its great head as it studied her. "She looks small."

"A tight fit gives the greatest pleasure."

The two of them talking about her in blunt sexual terms should have been infuriating. Instead it was . . . well . . . hot. Tension coiled and built low in her belly, sending an anticipatory thrumming through her body.

The dragon hmmed, then sent his tail winding around her bare leg. "You say she isn't virgin between her thighs. Where has she never known man?"

Kenric reached out to fondle her mound with casual familiarity, and her body reacted to his touch with an intensity that shocked her. She arched her pelvis to welcome his caress and invite more. He continued to stroke her pussy as he went on, "She's never spread her buttocks to receive a cock between them."

"How sweet." Kadar purred. "We'll break her in gently."

Kenric gave her pubic curls a last pet, finding her clit and fingering it deliberately in the process. The caress sent a jolt of sensation to her core, made her body throb with desire for his. Despite, or maybe because of, the fact that he was leaving her spread-eagled and bare for his friend.

Sybil drew in a breath, wondering if he was going to go further. He'd said they'd all have her, separately and together. The intensity of that encounter told her how much he liked the idea.

Kenric toyed with her breasts and watched as her body responded, back arching, nipples tightening. "Be good, witch, and the dragon might eat you."

Then he strode away, leaving her alone with the dragon.

"I think we've played enough with your dragon and damsel fantasy." Mist swirled and cleared to leave a bronze-haired naked man standing in front of her. The tail remained. Sybil glanced down at it, then back up at him. He shrugged. "You said you were willing to come to my bed. Did you think being taken by a dragon wouldn't be an exotic experience?"

"I didn't really think too much about the particulars," Sybil admitted in a hoarse voice. "I didn't notice the tail the last time I saw you naked."

"You were too busy checking out my front." Kadar gave her a knowing grin.

Sybil felt the serpentine tail sliding up and around her thigh until it reached behind her. The pointed end probed at the crease of her butt.

"A virgin ass," Kadar said. "I hope you know that won't last."

"I hope you know you won't fit in there," she muttered through dry lips.

"I'll fit myself anywhere I please," he informed her.

She felt her eyes go wide as that appendage moved unerringly to the right spot, pushing at the tight rosette, undulating in a coaxing caress. Her opening gave way under the pressure as the tip of his tail began to penetrate.

"Deliciously tight," Kadar said, his voice approving. "I'm so going to enjoy you."

The alien caress wasn't unpleasant. The point was nearly equal in thickness to the two fingers Kenric had worked into her. She blinked, remembering that. Had he been preparing her for this? If so, did that make him thoughtful of her, or of his friend?

"Poor Sybil, so confused." Kadar gave her a wicked grin as he toyed with her. "The steel and stone feel cold, but you're getting so hot. The man you've spent the last twenty-four hours with just gave you to another man. Being displayed like this for me turns you on. Your little nipples are all tight and hard and when Kenric stroked your pussy in front of me, you wanted him to go further."

She breathed unsteadily. "That's twisted."

"Is it? Why? Didn't you find pleasure in his bed?"

Sybil felt a wave of heat stain her cheeks. "Yes."

"Didn't it thrill you to have me see how much you liked the way he touched you? Didn't you enjoy me watching him touching you?"

"Uh." She couldn't deny that some part of her enjoyed being chained up for a strange man's pleasure, and had liked the way Kenric touched her intimately in front of an audience. She imagined him moving between her legs and sliding inside her while she was helpless, imprisoned, other eyes watching her performance, and felt a dizzying wave of sheer lust sweep over her.

"Why haven't you ever given in to your exhibitionist tendencies?"

Sybil blinked. "Ah. Um. You know, it's not exactly done."

Kadar caressed her anal opening in a rhythmic slide, watching her with knowing eyes. "Do you want me to call him back, so he can watch me make you come?"

"No!" Her sex clenched, her anus tightened, and the unaccustomed penetration there abruptly made delicate tissues blossom with unaccustomed sensation. "Oh!"

"Oh, yes." Kadar turned his head. "Kenric!"

"No, don't!" Her body reacted in a mixed rush of desire and panic.

Kadar laughed as he withdrew the tip of his tail. "I'm going to ride you while one of the others watches us before I let you go. And you'll enjoy it."

The idea excited her far more than it disturbed her. That in itself told her he was right. She stared at him in silence, not certain if she should dread the debauchery ahead or revel in it.

"Remember, Sybil, I know what you're thinking. I know what you really want. I know you nearly came at the idea of getting caught by your werewolf lover, naked and chained, while I toyed with your ass."

She nearly came now from his description. His low laugh was far too knowing. She glowered at him, and his smile widened.

"I'm pissing you off, and that makes you even hotter. I have you spreadeagled at my mercy. I can do anything I want to you, including calling in a crowd to watch me amusing myself with you or to join in. And you like that. You like knowing you're going to be shared with multiple men."

Sybil drew in a sharp breath as the impact of that hit home.

Kadar's face sobered. "You didn't know you had such forbidden desires. You've never acted on them, and a week ago you would have denied having them. You might even have believed you were telling the truth."

She didn't say anything. What was there to say?

"It's all right, Sybil." Kadar moved closer and cupped her cheek with one hand. "I like knowing you want this. I like knowing you want me, even while you still want Kenric so much your body aches for him."

She bit her lip and closed her eyes, feeling truly exposed now. She had no secrets.

"None," Kadar breathed in agreement. "I even know you

want me to take you just like this, standing between your open legs while I have you in chains."

His fingers threaded into her hair and stroked, his touch gentle and reassuring. "You're with a man who sees your thoughts and finds them erotic, enticing, pleasing. You have freedom to experience all you desire with partners who will offer even more than you dream of."

"And what if I like that too much?" She opened her eyes and met his. "What if I become addicted to sex with Kenric, with you, with all of you?"

"Addiction is destructive." He feathered a kiss along her brow, then down the curve of her cheek. "Did giving in to lust for the wolf hurt you?"

No. Yes. She hadn't expected to want him so urgently, so completely. Hadn't been ready for him to leave.

"Don't confuse feeling with weakness." Kadar's voice softened to a whisper as his lips brushed the corner of her mouth. "He marked you. You're bound to him. When it ends, you'll be bound to all of us. That's why you'll willingly return to our beds. And it's a two-way street, witch."

Oh. The realization made her eyes widen. Then Kadar's mouth moved over hers and her lashes fluttered down to rest against her cheeks.

eight

Being kissed by a dragon was like nothing she imagined. His lips were firm and sensual, sliding against hers with irresistible skill, coaxing them to first soften, then cling, then part and allow him to deepen the kiss. The tip of his tongue teased her until she opened wider to let it slide between her lips, explore the inner recesses of her mouth, search out her tongue and tease it into twining with his.

The mating of mouths made her breathing quicken and her breasts ache for his touch. Kadar let out a soft laugh and settled the hand that wasn't cupping her cheek over one breast. His thumb caressed her swollen nipple until she arched into his hand to gain more pressure there. He gave her a gentle squeeze, making her sigh into his mouth.

He stepped closer, letting his engorged penis ride between her open thighs. The ridge of his cock slid along her slick folds, an intimate caress that sent desire curling through her.

He knew exactly how good it felt, she realized, sliding her tongue along his while he echoed the action with the thick shaft stroking her sex. He knew the contact sent frissons of delight through her. Knew she was growing attuned to him, accepting him as a lover, anticipating the moment when he would part her labia and push inside, stretching her tissues wide as she strained to accommodate him.

"I know all that and more," Kadar murmured in a seductive voice. "I know you'd take pleasure in another lover readying your body for mine. You wanted Kenric to stay and stroke your sweet flesh until you were wet for me. You wanted me to watch his fingers pushing into you, opening you, preparing you to take me deep inside."

She couldn't deny that, so she didn't bother. She let her lips and tongue communicate on a more primal level while her body hummed with awareness of his.

His hands grew bolder, moving over her body, exploring curves and hollows and dips. He caressed the lower curve of her bare butt, the soft skin of her inner thighs, the slender rise of her ribs, and the sensitive nipples that pouted for more of his touch.

Kadar gradually ended the kiss, nibbling at her lower lip before dipping his head to attend to first one nipple, then the other, tasting her as if she were some exotic treat.

"You are, you know," he said against the skin between her breasts. "Not many witches around anymore."

"We're not that rare," Sybil protested.

He raised his head and stared into her eyes. She noticed for the first time that his pupils were slitted like a cat's.

"Sybil, the witches all but perished. The bloodline barely survived, thinned by intermarriage with nonmagical humans, diluted by atrophy as more forgot what they were with each generation."

She blinked. "How can that be true? I'm in a coven. Every witch in my family line always has been. We can't possibly be that rare."

His face sharpened with alarm. "Sybil, what coven? And do they have any way of keeping tabs on you?"

"I don't know what you mean."

"Show me."

Vulcan mind-meld, she thought giddily, and closed her eyes as she tried to picture the answers he wanted. Her mother's face, her grandmother's. The coven's high priestess and the other members. They numbered twelve, including her. She felt him probing at the memory of her mother and grandmother and brought up the image of a rain-slick bridge where a small car had gone skidding off. Grief welled up inside her all over again, and she broke away, shivering with loss.

"Shh. I'm sorry I made you remember that." Kadar enfolded her in his arms, cradling her close. She tried to hug him back and the chains creaked in protest.

"It's okay." She blinked away the stinging pressure in her eyes. "It was a long time ago."

"It was yesterday to your heart." He kissed the top of her head. "Sybil, you think you walked into danger by accident. The truth is, you escaped it by the skin of your teeth. You've been in danger all your life. The members of your coven weren't trying to protect you from doing harm. They were using you as demon bait."

"What?" Her head jerked up, barely missing clipping his chin. "What are you saying?"

Kadar released her to frame her face with his hands. "I'm saying they knew what you were and they've been waiting for this day for generations. By keeping your line ignorant, they've been able to keep you powerless. You may be the last true descendent of the first witch to possess the demon book, the only conduit it could use."

She stared at him in shock, shaking her head in useless denial. "That's not possible."

"Isn't it? They knew the book existed once, that it belonged to a witch, and that it held the key to unimaginable power. Power they could have if they had you."

She shook her head over and over and then realized she was trembling, cold all the way through.

Kadar made a low sound and let her go to unshackle her wrists and ankles. Then he swept her unresisting form up into his arms, cradling her against his broad chest. "I wanted you to play dragon's treasure the first time you saw my lair," he said, his tone deliberately light. "You're ruining my plans."

"S-sorry," she mumbled through chattering teeth.

"Idiot girl." He hugged her close, his indulgent tone making the insult an endearment. "You have nothing to be sorry for. Well, you should be sorry you missed getting gloriously screwed while naked and chained to a rock, but we'll make up for that later."

She let out a short laugh, then subsided into uncontrollable shivers that wracked her frame.

Kadar's lair was beautiful, decadent, exotic, and reminiscent of something out of the Arabian nights. Silk curtains hung around an enormous bed. Pillows scattered invitingly on the deep pile of an oriental rug. Colors and scents blended to create a sensual dream. She smelled citrus and spice and something enticing and unidentifiable.

"I knew you'd like it." Kadar smiled at her but his eyes

were worried. He settled her on the bed and stretched beside
her, pulling her into the curve of his body. He drew layers of
silk and velvet over her, wrapping her in warmth.

"You're being so nice to me," she muttered, burrowing into
him. "Thank you."

"You're naked in bed with me. Thank you," he returned.

She smiled and felt the chill of shock begin to thaw as he
enveloped her in an embrace that comforted her even as it
reminded her that she was, in fact, naked in bed with a strange
male. Who was still noticeably aroused.

"Dragons have legendary appetites," Kadar said, rocking
his hips to bump his penis against her belly. "We're also very
patient."

"You're very wonderful." She slithered up his body until
she could kiss him, her lips warming as they moved against his.

"I lied," he said in a strained voice when she finally ended
the kiss. "I'm not patient at all. I want you under me, naked
and splayed, and I want my cock inside you now."

Sybil reached down to gingerly explore the ridged, spined
extrusions around his penis. They gave at her touch, proving
flexible and surprisingly malleable. Not sharp or hard as she'd
expected.

"That won't hurt you," Kadar assured her. "Just the opposite."

She thought about where they would press once he was

deep within her and felt herself getting slick as she imagined the stimulation to her clit and labia. She circled his shaft with her hand, stroking his length as she measured him. "You're huge."

"You're elastic."

"There's a limit."

"I'll make you forget it."

Sybil wanted exactly that. Wanted him to make her forget everything in a white heat of lust.

Kadar rolled over with her, pushing her onto her back and coming to rest on top of her. His legs slid between hers and pushed them apart. He moved down until his mouth made contact with her clit, and Sybil's eyes closed as sensation washed over her.

His lips were warm and mobile, exploring her folds and searching out her secrets, uncovering every sensitive spot and applying just the right pressure with tongue and fingers in just the right combination.

He licked and suckled her sex until she was slick and eager, trembling with need, hips bucking in urgent invitation. Then he slowly filled her tight sheath with his fingers and worked them in and out while his teeth caught her clit, released it, suckled the sensitive bud, then laved it with his tongue. She thrashed in the broad bed, fisted her hands in folds of fabric, and came in a frenzy.

Kadar didn't let her drop from the peak he'd sent her to.

He covered her body with his and aligned the head of his shaft with her opening while she was still quivering with after-shocks of pleasure. "That's it," he murmured, rocking himself forward and sending the head pushing between her slick folds. "Take my cock inside your soft, sweet pussy."

Her inner muscles clenched involuntarily but her tightness proved no barrier to his determined thrust.

"You're so wide," she muttered, letting her lashes flutter up so she could meet his exotic eyes.

"You're so wet and ready," he countered, working his way deeper as her flesh stretched around his girth. "You loved my tongue in you but it wasn't enough, was it? My fingers weren't enough, either. Your sweet pussy aches to be filled with cock."

Sybil groaned at his graphic words and the erotic invasion of her flesh. "Yes," she admitted. "I want you to fill me."

"I'll stuff you so full you can't move," Kadar promised. He slid deeper, pushed harder, and then his head reached all the way to her womb. Her sex stretched to capacity and Sybil teetered on the edge between pleasure and pain. She felt his ridged flesh make contact with her clitoris and the additional stimulation overloaded her senses.

"Kadar." She tried to breathe, tried to relax herself under him, around him.

"Sybil," he murmured. "Your silky pussy is so sensitive. My shaft is so wide, so warm. When I move inside you it's like a deep massage, finding every pressure point, stimulating every nerve."

"Mmm," she agreed, cautiously tilting her pelvis to meet his slow stroke. More of those extrusions met her pleasure-swollen labia and she groaned at the contact.

"It feels incredible to be inside you." He nuzzled her cheek. "Spread wider. Wrap your legs around me. Give me more."

"Greedy dragon." She was greedy, too, though, so she strained to opened her thighs wider and wound her legs around his waist, bringing her hips up to make a cradle for him to rock in and out of.

"Take my cock," Kadar growled. "All of it. Again. And again." He searched out her lips and slid his tongue between them. He rode her with shallow thrusts as if he couldn't bear to withdraw more than an inch or two from the silken grip of her sex before pushing back into her depths. His head pressed at the entrance of her womb with each stroke, making her groan at the deep sensation of pressure while the external stimulation drove her wild.

His tongue mated with hers as he rocked into her again and again. She forgot how to breathe. She forgot everything but the indescribable pleasure that built and built. Her inner muscles spasmed as her orgasm took her, and the silken squeeze made Kadar's cock jerk in response. His shaft swelled, jerked again, and then hot liquid jetted against her inner walls while she moaned and writhed under him, coming in an endless wave. He thrust harder, roaring his release, pumping into her with viscous spurts that went on and on.

"Sweet witch," Kadar growled when he came to rest on top of her. "Sweet pussy, taking every inch of my cock and every drop of my come."

"That should be disgusting," Sybil mumbled. "Why does hearing you talk like that make me feel excited all over again?"

"Because you lust after me." He pushed himself up on his elbows to give her a knowing look. "I'm hot and you want me. Hearing that I lust after you makes you feel desirable and sexy. I want you feeling sexy and desirable. It maximizes my chances of fucking you again."

"You have to," she pointed out. "You didn't mark me."

"I couldn't the first time." He withdrew slowly, carefully, then rolled on his back and reached for her. He settled her on top of him, her limbs splayed in an abandoned sprawl. "You weren't comfortable enough with me to take anal penetration at the same time."

Sybil touched the tattoo on his chest with tentative fingers. "With the tip of your tail? Is that required?"

"Yes."

"That's . . ."

"Hot." Kadar pulled her into kissing range, claiming her

mouth with hard, hungry demand. "You're going to come so hard you might go blind."

She let out a squeak of alarm, or maybe anticipation, and then for a long time the only sounds that escaped his mouth were her soft moans and sighs.

"Thank you," Sybil said in a soft voice when she could talk again. "You made me feel safe." He'd also made her feel wanted.

"You are safe with me." Kadar stroked her back and the round swells of her buttocks. "You're safe with all of us."

"Except for the sadistic elf," she muttered.

"It's his way of showing he cares."

"He could say it with flowers."

"You may come to appreciate his way."

She huffed a breath against his bare chest. "Not likely."

"You really are afraid of him." Kadar's amusement soured her mood.

"It's not funny." Sybil wiggled free of his grip and tried to climb off. He caught her easily and pulled her back, settling her thighs on either side of his hips so her sex rested against his thick shaft.

"Yes, it is. The most powerful witch in centuries quakes at the thought of going to bed with a member of a race known for their sexual prowess. Mating with the fae can make flowers bloom, oceans rise."

"Bruises bloom. Welts rise." She huddled against Kadar's chest in an unhappy heap. "He's going to hurt me and the rest of you are going to let him."

"I think you're more afraid that you'll like it than you are of anything Ronan might do to you."

"I don't want to talk about him anymore." She rocked back and forth, sending her sex sliding along the length of his cock.

"Coward."

"Beast."

"I'm a greedy beast who wants your flesh," Kadar agreed. "Are you prepared to surrender to the lust of a dragon?"

"Yes." She wanted him to mark her. She wanted to know the exquisite sensation of his cock inside her again, filling her so completely there was no room for anything else. She wanted to experience the wicked pleasure of that pointed tail of his penetrating her anus while her vulva was stretched to the limit from his width, his head probing the entrance of her womb as she strained to take his length.

The air thickened and magic pulsed around them, the beat of it making her body throb in time.

"You want me bad." Kadar laughed out loud and she felt his tail wind around her thigh.

"That thing is obscene," she murmured. And wiggled her ass in blatant invitation.

"It's perfectly normal for my species. And you liked it."

"I did," she admitted, remembering that burst of pleasure unlike anything she'd very experienced.

She felt the point of his tail exploring the tight, puckered opening between her buttocks, stroking and stimulating hidden nerves. Then there was a sensation of pressure, her body giving way to it, and that first shock of penetration as the tip worked into her ass. She sucked in a sharp breath as he probed deeper. A shock of magic sang through her body.

"We'll work with that," Kadar said. "Soon, when you're riding astride with your hot ass in the air, you'll be ready to take a second cock, and two of us can have you at once."

"What makes you think I'll want that?" Sybil asked, arching her lower back to offer more of herself to his invading member.

He merely smiled.

She made an inarticulate sound as he continued his ministrations, astonished at her own appetite for sex. Kenric had taken her until she was utterly spent, handed her off to the next man in linc, and now here she was eagerly mounting him for round two.

"It's magic," Kadar said, reading her thought. "You committed yourself to the service of a sex goddess and took the first mark. You'll crave the second, the third, the fourth, and the fifth. You'll be insatiable until the ritual is complete."

Insatiable? For all of them?

"Take me now," he gritted out, pushing up into her and derailing thought. He gripped her hips and pulled her down on top of him, seating himself deep inside her body.

She moaned as he withdrew, thrust deep, withdrew again, and stroked the full length of himself into her tight sheath. Again. And again. The pressure in her anus added to the sensation of having her sex stretched to the limit, making her even fuller, utterly possessed by him. Magic built in waves each time they moved together until she felt lost in the spell.

"Kadar."

"I have you." He released one hip to move his hand over her naked torso as she rocked with the rhythm of his thrusts.

She cried out at the added stimulation, writhing and throwing her head back as she fought to ride the wave of sensation sweeping her away.

He held her fast, drove into her harder, taking her with relentless lust.

"Kadar. I can't take it."

"You can take all of it. I'm going to come, and you'll take that, too. Take me, witch."

He pushed deeper between her legs as he played the tender opening between her buttocks, making her scream as the force of her orgasm wracked her. He roared out his own pleasure and came with a frenzy that matched hers as a surge of magic released.

Nine

I think you killed me," Sybil whispered a long time later. Her voice had cracked from screaming her satisfaction while she ground herself against the erotically designed base of his cock. It was some consolation that Kadar's voice was reduced to a husky whisper after the dragon-worthy roar he'd let out.

If any of the others were on the same planet, they'd heard him coming. She winced, imagining the reactions.

He chuckled. "Envy," he assured her. "And you're not dead. You're still talking."

"In whispers. My throat is raw."

"Your throat is sexy. I want to nibble on it."

He suited action to words, making her squirm and shake with helpless, silent giggles.

"Sexy witch." His mouth moved lower, licked at the mark now two-fifths complete on her breast. "This looks good on you."

His lips soothed the brand. Then they closed around her nipple and sucked. He released the tight bud and laved it with his tongue as if he found the taste of her addictive.

"I do," he growled. "I want to feast on your nipples, then spread you wide and lick you between your legs until you come all over my tongue."

"I don't think I can come any more. Ever. For the rest of my life."

"That's a shame, because I'm not done coming in you, and I'll enjoy it more if you come, too."

"But you'll still enjoy it if I don't."

"That goes without saying." Kadar wrestled her down and pinned her body with his. "It's not possible to bury my cock in you and not enjoy it."

"You can't possibly still be hard." She gaped at him and he laughed, then kissed her with rough lust.

"You make me hard. Hold still, witch, I need to fuck you again."

"You really are going to kill me."

His mouth took hers. She opened for it, and then his body took hers once more. He was patient and thorough and when he came again, she came with him. When she slid into sleep her limbs were still twined with his and his arms were wrapped protectively around her as if she was a treasure he guarded.

sybil eased away from Kadar's sleeping form and scooted to a sitting position on the bed. He made a low sound when she moved, but didn't wake. She drew her knees to her chest and curled her arms around them as she stared at nothing.

She could feel the difference in the expanded mark that was now four points of a star, halfway complete. It almost hummed under her skin like two notes of a chord. Abaran and Adrian would finish the job, and Ronan would enclose it in the circle.

The thought of Ronan made her shiver.

"Cold?" Kadar came awake and reached for her, pulled her back down and ran his hands over her naked form. "I'll warm you."

"Stop that. I can't possibly do you again," Sybil complained, batting at his hands.

"Why not? Are you hurt?" He frowned and rose up on one elbow to study her from a better angle. "Witch, where is the pain?"

"Nowhere. I'm not hurt. I'm fine."

"You had better be fine. I can't have an unhappy woman in my bed. I have a reputation to uphold. They all leave smiling and satisfied. If you aren't fine, I'll be forced to make you come screaming again."

She snorted. "You're such a giver."

"I may have to give you something." He gave her a one-armed hug that let her feel just what he'd give her. "What woke you? If anyone has upset you, I'll kill them and bring you their dismembered parts."

She pictured a cat depositing bloody trophies at her doorstep and bit her lip as she fought to hide a grin. "Nobody upset me."

"So you claim." He reclined with her in his arms and cradled the back of her head in one hand as he guided her cheek to his shoulder. "Tell me," he invited out loud.

"You'll laugh at me."

"I'm not laughing." He stroked he back, soothing her. "How could I laugh at anything that upset you?"

She was silent. Then she whispered a name. "Ronan."

"Your fear of him is unreasonable."

"He's going to hurt me." An involuntary tremor shook her. "And I'll have to let him."

"Sybil." He hugged her tight. "You aren't afraid of him. You're afraid of yourself."

"And it won't just be once," she went on as if he hadn't

spoken. "Once his, always his. I'll have to go back to him again and again for more."

He blew out a breath that held a hint of smoke. "If he makes your existence a misery, I will put a stop to it. But Ronan is one of us, and I have a feeling you'll find his proclivities . . . very stimulating. He is a Shadow Guardian, just like Kenric and I. Did you find anything I did unpleasant?"

"No." Far from it. Kadar approached sex like a sport. Earning aerobic points had never been so fun. He almost made her feel athletic.

"Did Kenric displease you?"

She felt a flash of emotion she did her best to hide. "No. Nothing like that."

His voice gentled, telling her he'd picked up on the feeling she had no words for. "How was sex with him?"

Sex with Kenric was shattering. She could fracture into a thousand shards just from the memory. "Um. The knot took me by surprise. Not that I'm complaining."

"He knotted you?" Kadar's hold tightened and at the same time turned very careful, as if she might be made of glass.

"I didn't mind." She'd lost her damn mind. The wolf had claimed her and fucked her mindless and now she couldn't hold two coherent thoughts.

"You wanted him before you agreed to let us mark you. But to be truly his means accepting the rest of us as a package deal." Kadar paused, then said, "No doubt he expressed his opinion of witches once or twice."

"I have no use for witches." Sybil mimicked Kenric's tone deadpan and wondered why his words held so much power to hurt. But they did, a twisting pain that cut so deeply it shocked her.

"Well, witches did kill him. And his entire pack. He took that hard. As the alpha, it was his duty to protect them. Actually, it was more like his reason for being."

She drew in a sharp breath. "Oh."

"Killed me and mine, too," the dragon volunteered.

She winced. "Anybody else?"

"All five of us and our armies fell before the united power of the witches and the demons from the shadow realm. The witches were our allies, but they turned on us to gain the book. We didn't suspect treachery. We were taken by surprise."

"Oh." Sybil went very still. "When I asked Kenric about the book, he mentioned something about a bargain witches made. He didn't mention he was there. Or died because of it."

"It was seeing his people slaughtered he can't forgive, I think."

She let out a shaky breath. "So Kenric hates me and the demon book I rode in on."

Kadar patted her bare butt. "I doubt he hates you. But he very likely hates the memories you're stirring up."

"Great." Her tone said the opposite.

"Forget the past. Focus on the present. You should kiss me again."

She did, a tentative caress that he coaxed into open-mouthed abandon. Then he ended the kiss, swept her up in his arms, and bounded out of bed with her.

"Come on, witch. I know what you need."

"You do?" Sybil asked, blatantly suspicious, but she curled an arm around his neck and leaned into him.

"I do. You need fresh air, exercise, the wind in your hair."

"The wind . . . oh, no, Kadar."

"Oh, yes."

Minutes later, Sybil wound her arms around his scaled, serpentine neck in a death grip. Her legs clamped his sides. His wings unfurled behind her. His talons gripped the edge of a rock precipice above a plunging abyss.

"I'm going to be sick," she moaned.

"Sissy witch. Afraid to fly," Kadar taunted.

"Witches don't fly."

"And you know this because you've spent so much time among them?"

"Witches don't fly," she repeated, less certainly this time. "Those are just stories."

"Stories were once called history." With that, the dragon launched them both into space.

Kadar was yanking her chain. And goddess knew he loved doing it. She decided to yank back. "What's the deal with you and your kinky tail, anyway? Is it sort of like an extra hand?"

"Exactly. In my man form it's a vestigial characteristic, but a lot more fun than your appendix."

"Oh." That was one way to look at it.

"Dead tree on that rock outcropping to your left," Kadar called. "Set it on fire."

"Excuse me?"

"Target practice," the cheerful answer rang out. "Let's test your range."

"I don't have range." She tightened her grip on him. "I can't even light a candle unless I have a match."

"You made a spark. Kenric noted your progress."

"You guys really think I can control this?"

"With time and training, yes. Also, you need the full seal of the goddess to keep the demon's spells contained and under your command." Kadar's head curled back so one jeweled eye could fix on her. "Did you think we would make you one of our number as a joke? The witches were our allies once. Your power can serve more than your own ends."

And would that make up for a betrayal of the past? "Watch where you're flying," Sybil said, her voice tight.

"What, like this?" He swooped low, making her stomach

drop; soared up, and looped backward while she clung tight and screamed. "You're doing it wrong. Hands up in the air!"

"Crazy dragon!"

"Fraidy witch." He dove toward the tree he'd indicated. "Light it on fire, or I'll do a double loop next time."

Fire. Okay. That was an element, which meant it was already there, she just had to call it. It was popping out all the damn time without her doing a thing anyway, so how hard could it be? She stared at a tree and thought, *burn.*

Smoke bloomed. Moments later, flame licked along the dead branches with an audible crackle.

"Holy shit," Sybil whispered.

"That's my girl." His tail swept forward and stroked her bare leg. "Let's do it again."

He swooped, soared, dove, and called out a series of targets. She couldn't manage to make so much as a puff of smoke after her first success, and her frustration mounted as her energy ebbed.

"Enough," Kadar said. "You're so tired you slipped on that last turn." He circled and caught an updraft that sent them soaring back. He landed with his wings extended like parachutes, then folded them neatly back. "Down you go."

Sybil half-slid, half-fell off and landed on her butt. He picked her up with his forelegs and carried her as he made his way back to his lair. "I'm too heavy," she protested.

"I can carry cattle."

"Okay, I'm not *that* heavy."

Kadar laughed. He released her as he passed the rock she'd been manacled to. "Follow me."

She did, and discovered that in addition to his opulent bed chamber, he had a deep tub that looked like marble. "Is that faucet gold?"

"Do dragons collect cheap imitations?"

"Wow." Sybil touched it with a hesitant fingertip.

"Gold is precious, but jewels are better." He nodded toward the tub. "And that reminds me of something. Get in. I'll be right back."

She didn't have to be told twice. The luxurious bath was big enough to swim in, which made sense, given Kadar's size. In both forms. She found scented bath salts in a gold container and poured a handful under the jet of water that appeared when she turned a gold tap.

By the time Kadar returned in man form, she'd washed thoroughly, rinsed her hair, and was soaking in blissful relaxation.

"Over here, witch."

"I have a name," she said, but scooted to the side of the tub he approached.

"I know. It's lovely." Kadar bent to kiss her, continued to explore the curves of her lips and taste the inner recesses of her mouth as he climbed in to join her, then pulled her down onto his lap to get serious about it. He kissed her with single-minded concentration, expertise, and cheerful lust. The result left her pulse thudding and her body tingling. "Bend your head."

She did, and he opened his hand to let a delicate chain slide from his palm to dangle by one finger. "What's that?"

"A present." He fastened the chain at the nape of her neck and straightened the tear-shaped pendant so that it settled between her breasts. "Diamonds may not be a girl's best friend, but they never hurt."

She sucked in a breath. "Kadar, that's a diamond? What'd you do, break into the Smithsonian?"

He laughed. "It isn't the Hope diamond, although it's nearly as large. I came by it honestly and now it's yours."

Sybil touched the brilliant surface that glittered like cold fire and felt it sing to the fire inside her. "It's not just a gem, is it?"

"No. It came from the fae's realm. Old magic. It's a focus, to help you direct your power."

The size of the rock alone made it priceless. The magical value had to be insane.

"If you want to think about the price, think about what it would cost all of us if you fell into the wrong hands," Kadar said. "You need this and I want you to have it. You may thank me."

"Thank you." Her voice sounded as faint as she felt.

"I had something more athletic and less verbal in mind, actually."

Sybil laughed. "I'll bet."

"You need pampering first, though. You'll need your strength." His eyes gleamed with intent and she felt her sex react.

Kadar's idea of building up her strength included a leisurely bath. Afterward he had her lay on a length of linen while he massaged her with scented oil from head to toe, not missing any part of her and paying special attention to some. He smoothed it along her buttocks, parted them and coated her anus, then worked a tiny amount inside while she rested on her belly.

When she shifted onto her back, he applied it generously to her nipples and her sex after he'd attended to her arms, belly, hips, throat, and legs. Then he took his time making certain her folds were slick with oil, sliding his fingers into her sheath to extend the lubrication.

"Kadar," she murmured, her voice hitching as he worked his hand between her thighs.

Soon he led her back to the stone Kenric had shackled her to. She raised her arms and allowed him to fasten the manacles around her wrists, slid her feet wide apart, and watched as he captured her ankles, imprisoning her.

"How does that feel?" Kadar asked, looking up at her.

Depraved. Exciting. "Fine."

"You look like a treasure fit for a dragon," he informed her. "Naked and glistening. Breasts upthrust for the enjoyment of any male who finds you like this. Your body slick and soft and ready." He petted her pubic mound as he spoke. "Anybody could see you. Anybody could touch those rosy nipples. Reach between your legs to sink their fingers into your sweet flesh. Kneel to take a taste of your honey. Stand to mount you."

She was breathing faster, nipples tight and pouting, her sex aching for more.

Kadar stood, walked around to admire her from all sides, caressed her hip, smoothed his palm over her breast. "So soft, so lovely."

So ready. What was he waiting for?

He kissed her, a scorching demand she met and returned. His hand found its way between her thighs and cupped her sex. As his tongue slid into her mouth, his fingers thrust inside her. She moaned against his lips. The kiss went on and on. His hand worked her flesh with seductive skill as he thumbed her clit, ground his palm against her mound, pushed his fingers deeper into her sheath, and twisted them inside her.

He broke the kiss to turn his head toward the entrance. "Be with you in a moment."

Sybil's breath froze, her eyes opening wide and going from

Kadar's face to the entrance, where they locked with Abaran's heated gaze.

The dark demon looked even more muscular than she remembered, his bare, sculpted torso and arms gleaming above the leather pants that molded themselves to his lower half. His shaved head added an aggressive edge to his appearance. Everything about him spelled threat. The ultimate bad boy of reckless sexual fantasies.

Apparently she harbored a reckless fantasy or two, because her nipples hardened and her sex throbbed while she stared into his fathomless midnight eyes.

"Come for me," Kadar breathed as he bent his head to kiss the soft skin behind her ear. "He's watching us. Looking at you. Show him what he has to look forward to."

"I can't," she whispered back, but he stroked a sensitive spot deep inside her while his other hand moved up to tease her nipples and her breathing hitched. Kadar increased the pressure on that hidden spot and she trembled.

It was twisted to find this so exciting. To love getting caught with Kadar's hand between her legs while she was naked and spread open.

"Not at all." Kadar answered her thought as he moved to the side so that her body was better displayed for Abaran while he continued to pleasure her with his hand. "You like having his eyes on you while I'm touching you. You like being exposed and unable to do anything about it. He's watching me push my fingers into you and imagining it's his cock you're taking."

She let out a soft moan.

"You look so pretty, all flushed and eager, legs apart, riding my hand." Kadar kissed the curve of her shoulder, careful not to block Abaran's view. "You're even more beautiful when you come. Yes, that's it."

His low-voiced encouragement combined with the hot delight of what he was doing to her sent her over the edge. She moaned again and jerked helplessly in her manacles while her hips bucked, grinding herself against his hand.

Kadar slowly withdrew his fingers, stroked her sex as he gave her another deep kiss, then left her hanging there, naked, exposed, still almost unbearably aroused.

He conferred with Abaran, their voices pitched too low for her to hear. She waited, torn between embarrassment and satisfaction.

The two men finished, and walked toward her. She swallowed hard and wondered what would happen next. Abaran reached out to cup her breasts, as if testing their weight and firmness. "Very nice."

Her body jolted at the first touch of his hands. She looked into his eyes and said nothing, intensely aware of herself as a sexual being, equally aware of him. Wanting whatever came next.

He pinched her nipples between his thumbs and forefingers and she sucked in a breath at the firm pressure. His hands felt hotter, as if his body temperature ran higher, and the texture of his skin felt almost like he wore fine leather gloves. He tugged and the stimulation went straight to her sex.

"Sensitive," he added in an approving tone. He released his pinching hold on her taut peaks and ran his hands over her torso, making her nerves sing everywhere he touched her.

"She's wonderfully responsive," Kadar said, giving her bare hip an appreciative caress. The sensation of having two men touching her made her weak with desire. "Stroke her clit just so and she nearly comes out of her skin."

"Does she?"

"See for yourself." Kadar grinned and Sybil fought not to squirm and reveal her level of excitement. Abaran cupped the palm of his hand between her legs. He met her eyes and held them as he gave her an intimate squeeze, then ran his fingertip just inside the seam of her labia, not quite penetration but, oh goddess, he was doing it in front of Kadar, who was offering her up to him like a gift.

Abaran drew his fingertip over her clit in a slow, drawn-out movement and she whimpered at the jolt of sensation. His face grew sharp with hunger. "I'm going to love taking my turn with you," he said. He turned his head to Kadar. "I saw how much she enjoyed your hand between her legs. How did she like your cock?"

Kadar grinned, his teeth flashing white. "I'll show you."

His earlier claim that he'd take her in front of an audience before he let her go rang in her ears. He was actually going to. And she had no choice but to let him.

ten

S ybil gasped as Abaran stepped back and Kadar moved to stand between her parted legs. He wrapped one hand around his thick shaft and guided it into position, until he was pressing against her opening. Her flesh gave way easily to allow his head entry, betraying her eagerness.

He was going to fuck her while she was helpless in chains and Abaran stood by, watching. She was going to die. She was going to come instantly.

"That's it. Open your sweet pussy for me," Kadar said, working more of himself in. He bent his head to kiss her, filling her mouth with his tongue as he slowly filled her with his insistent penis. He was hard, thick, demanding, irresistible. In this position it was all she could do to accommodate him, and she understood the reason for the lubricant he'd spread liberally over her mound and worked into her folds. Without it, she might not have been able to stretch around his size. With it, she was stuffed so full she couldn't move.

He rocked back and forth, giving her more of himself with each stroke, until he was in as far as their angle allowed and she was trembling and straining against her chains. She felt his tail wrap around her thigh, and quivered, knowing what was coming.

The pointed tip searched out her anus and pushed inside so hard it burned. She let out a hoarse cry at the dual invasion that had her so incredibly stretched to the limit that every sensation was magnified.

Kadar's tongue mated with hers. His pelvis rocked into her, sending his shaft deeper. She felt his penis throb, a telling reaction that meant his orgasm wasn't far off.

This wasn't going to last long, Sybil realized dimly, and that was good because she couldn't last. She was writhing and letting out helpless cries as Kadar impaled her with his thick shaft, the pleasure so intense she couldn't contain it. Abaran was watching it all, seeing and hearing her uninhibited response that revealed how much she loved the treatment Kadar was giving her. Loved having an audience for this intimate performance. Loved taking every inch Kadar could cram into her.

Her body bowed and broke as she came, and Kadar let out a roar of satisfaction, fucking her harder, ejaculating in a violent spending.

She sagged as her muscles went slack, letting the manacles and Kadar's body support her.

He let out a low, pleased laugh and ground his pelvis into hers, pressing those wicked ridges against her vulva. "That's how she likes it," he said over his shoulder to Abaran as he reached up to roll one of her nipples between his fingers.

Abaran moved closer and cupped her buttock, giving it a squeeze. "The witch enjoys the way you use your appendage, I see."

Kadar grinned at him. "I think you'll find each other to your mutual liking."

He gave Sybil another deep, hard kiss, grinding his lips against hers while he stayed planted in her body. "I hate to leave you, witch."

Her eyes widened as she caught his meaning. "Kadar?"

"Time's up." He pulled out of her by inches, drawing out the moment when their locked flesh would separate. When his head slid free of her, she felt bereft of his support. With him, she could face Abaran and be brave. Without him, she felt more chicken than confident erotic playmate. She made a soft sound of protest, unable to stop herself.

"Ah, don't fret." Kadar stood back, his spent penis laying against his thigh, still impressively thick. "Abaran will give you a fine ride."

She looked away, not wanting him to see the flicker of panic in her eyes. How was she going to go through with this? After the porn star display she'd put on, Abaran would think she'd be comfortable with anything. And when he put his hands on her again, maybe she would be. She was losing her boundaries, losing herself with these men.

Kadar moved forward again until his body pressed hers into the rock behind her. He whispered for her ears only, "Losing yourself? Or finding yourself?"

Abaran slid his arm between them, pushing Kadar back. He gave Sybil a look so fierce she would have stumbled if she'd been standing under her own power. "Do you refuse me?"

"What?" She stared at him, confused.

"Do you refuse me?" Abaran repeated the words slowly and clearly. "Do you refuse to come to my bed?"

Sybil felt her cheeks flushing scarlet. "No. I mean, not no. I'm not refusing. I . . ." she ground to a halt, mired in verbal quicksand and sinking fast.

"Ease up," Kadar said to Abaran. "Our little witch is

sensitive all the way through and you're scaring her." He caressed the curve of her cheek and directed his next words to her. "You are a treasure to be shared, not hoarded. It is time I let you go. Abaran has been patient long enough."

"Abaran could be more patient," the demon said in a gruff tone. He relaxed the arm he'd made into a barrier between Sybil and Kadar, drawing back to stroke her bare belly in an inviting gesture. "It might ease the transition if we shared her between us before I take her from you."

"Would you like that?" Kadar stroked her cheek lightly once again and then rubbed his knuckles along her jawbone as he asked her the question.

She pictured herself bracketed by both naked men. Kneeling to wrap her lips around Kadar's shaft while the other man moved into position behind her . . . Sybil swallowed and found her voice again. "No. Thank you, Abaran, that's a generous offer, but if it's time, we should go."

"She wants it," Kadar told the other man. "She just doesn't want to interfere with your time and your choice."

He left out the fact that she was too chicken to act on the fantasy, which Sybil appreciated. Or maybe he was just confident that they could seduce her into trying it.

"Good of her." Abaran gave her a considering look that sent a shiver of something other than apprehension through her. Interest. Anticipation. Desire. "This position limits too many options, but it might be interesting for foreplay."

The two men on either side of her suddenly made her feel like a bird between two cats. Both of them ran their hands over her breasts, making her nipples and her pulse react to the uniform caress from two different partners. Abaran's hand moved lower until he cupped her sex with a possessive grip.

"You're softer just after you've been taken," he said, sinking his fingertips into her folds. "Still ready, and so slick you could take more without any resistance."

Sybil closed her eyes, imagining his shaft pressing inside her opening, sliding easily into her pleasure-softened flesh until she held all of him. His fingertips moved lower, testing her, pushing until three of his fingers were fitted tightly in her sheath.

Abaran exploited her response, working her with his hand while Kadar laved her nipples with his tongue and her body coiled tight. He watched her through half-lidded eyes and she found she couldn't look away from his dark gaze. "Will you come with my hand between your legs while the dragon looks on?"

Her breath hitched and she realized she was on the verge of doing just that. Climaxing like a wanton while Abaran filled her sex with his fingers. He rubbed the pad of his thumb over her clit and she let out a moan, unable to hide her response. He repeated the caress, drawing it out, drinking in her reaction, watching her hips raise for him while her torso arched to offer her breasts to Kadar's wicked mouth.

"Or maybe I'll move between your legs so I can teach you whose cock you should spread for now," said Abaran. "Drive inside you and make you come wrapped around my shaft."

Sybil felt a tremor run through her. Part of her wanted him to take her like this, rough and fast. His eyes gleamed and she realized they weren't truly black, but a purplish blue as deep as midnight. He looked like the demon lover of old stories, something born of darkness and old terrors and secret desires.

"Please," she whispered, not knowing if she asked him to do what he'd suggested or to wait.

"Please?" Abaran's expression grew feral. He released her to use both hands to unfasten his pants. He didn't strip them off, just freed the straining member that Sybil stared at, captivated. His penis curved in a shape reminiscent of a scimitar. He moved to stand between her legs and planted his palms against the rock on either side of her head as if preparing to do pushups from a standing position. Kadar shifted aside to make her more accessible.

Sybil had to ask the question. "Is that going to hurt?"

Abaran's smile widened. "Wait and see."

Not exactly reassuring, but Kadar was close, and she trusted him.

She felt the first heated contact of male flesh to female, as Abaran's penis slid along her labia like an introduction. She drew in a sharp breath, her eyes caught and held by his, waiting for him to possess her.

He found her entry, and pushed slowly, steadily inside while her senses reeled from the intimate exploration by an unfamiliar male. The curved shape of his shaft put more pressure in exactly the right places. His body pressed hers back, the rough surface of the rock abrading her buttocks, his hard, smooth chest flattening her breasts. His hot, leather-like flesh covered her and sent unexpected jolts of pleasure through her.

"I'm inside you," he said in a voice thick with satisfaction. "But not as deep as I'm going to go the next time I take you. I'll have you on your back with your knees over my shoulders. I'll have you on your knees with your ass raised high. I'll have you every way I want you. Over and over."

He withdrew, then rocked back into her as he spoke, his powerful muscles flexing as he drew out the slow, steady penetration. "Whose cock are you taking, witch?"

She swallowed convulsively, lost in exquisite sensation as he pushed all the way inside until his groin ground into hers. "Yours."

"Say my name."

"Abaran." She moaned the answer.

He turned his head to look at Kadar. "Free her."

Sybil wanted to scream in frustration when Abaran abruptly pulled out. He stood aside and waited while Kadar loosed her, then pulled her into his arms with her back to his chest, his penis cushioned by her buttocks. Kadar ran his hands up her ribs to cup her breasts, offering them to Abaran. The demon bent his head to suckle each in turn while Sybil's breath came harsher and faster.

Abaran's mouth scorched her sensitized peaks, the hard suction he applied making her whimper. Having Kadar hold her while another man ravished her flesh added an erotic edge to the experience.

"Told you you'd want it," Kadar murmured, his lips brushing her earlobe. "It feels so good to be in my arms while he tastes your sweet curves. You loved having him watch while I thrust between your legs. And you're going to love having me watch while he pushes into your slick heat next, your body still soft from coming for me."

She shivered, knowing what he meant. Being taken by two men at once. One in front. One behind. "Kadar, I don't think I can do it."

"Shh." He kissed the soft spot below her ear, nuzzled her neck. "Don't think. Just feel. Feel how much pleasure we can offer you."

Abaran raised his head to look into her eyes. "You're mine now, witch. I can do anything I wish with you."

She gulped audibly. She trembled and her knees sagged.

"Don't be afraid," Kadar said, stroking a hand down her side in a leisurely caress that made her nerve endings sing.

"Be afraid." Abaran bent his head to claim her lips in a hungry, bruising kiss. His tongue probed at her lips, demanding entry. When she opened at the pressure, his tongue filled her mouth. The taste of him made her gasp. Sinfully dark and delicious, his tongue against hers a seductive intimacy

When he ended the kiss, her lips were swollen and parted, her breath coming in pants while she stared at him with wide eyes.

He was a demon and he'd made her want him. He'd made her love the slide of his flesh into hers, the feel of his skin against hers, the sweet thrill of his mouth on her breasts and the harsh insistence of his lips grinding into hers while she opened to taste him and let him taste her.

Eleven

I like that look in your eyes." Abaran's mouth curved in satisfaction just before it crushed hers again, devouring her with a harsh, open kiss. His lips ground hers against her teeth while his tongue thrust inside, then withdrew. "That look that says you know you're mine now, and you don't trust me."

He shaped his palms over her breasts and squeezed, a rough caress that would have hurt if she'd been less aroused. A tremor wracked her frame and she leaned into Kadar's support. She felt his thick shaft stir against her and swallowed at the obvious state of his arousal. Abaran laughed at her reaction and raised his head to look past her at Kadar.

"Oh, she is delicious. So hot. So anxious. I don't know if she's afraid I'll make her take both of us at once, or afraid I won't."

Both. Sybil shivered and imagined the two of them piercing her body, her tender flesh burning as two cocks tunneled into her with ruthless lust.

"I don't know what I want more," Abaran went on as he pressed his body against hers. "To put you on your hands and knees and sink my cock into your pussy while Kadar fucks your mouth, or to push into your hot, tight ass while you take his cock between your thighs."

He ran his hand down her body in a brutally erotic caress. "Or maybe what I want most is to have you all to myself and at my mercy."

"Your choice," Kadar said. He stroked her arms, gentling her. "If you wish to share, I'll enjoy your generosity. If you wish to have her alone, you'll enjoy her undivided attention."

"And what do you say, witch?" Abaran stared into her eyes, demanding a response.

"Don't hurt me." The whisper escaped her before she could stop herself.

"Don't hurt you?" He shook his head and sank the edge of his teeth into her lower lip. "I can't promise that. There are so many kinds of hurt. You're hurting me now. My balls hurt from wanting to spend myself in you. My muscles hurt from restraint."

"Restraint?" She was afraid to ask, but she did, anyway.

"If I let myself touch you the way I want to, you might refuse to be alone with me."

"Take her," Kadar said. "You're too lost to instinct to share. When you've marked her, if you still want to experience her between us, call me and I'll come."

"I didn't think I'd have so little control," the demon said in a rough voice. "But she's a witch, and she smells of sex and demon power."

"Have a care with her," Kadar cautioned as he pushed her into Abaran's hands and stepped back. The fact that mind-reading Kadar felt the warning was needed made her swallow hard and tears stung the corners of her eyes.

Abaran caught her betraying reaction and his expression turned fierce. "You're mine. Are you afraid to come with me?"

"Yes." She licked dry lips, still bruised and swollen from his kisses. "Let's go."

His brows shot up. "Brave creature."

Oh, if only she was. But if she couldn't be brave, she could at least be fair. She reached a shaking hand up to touch his chest and trace the tattoo that shone against his skin. "If you're willing to give me the mark, I should be willing to take it from you. You didn't have to help me. You didn't have to put yourself in danger because of me."

His hand rose to cover hers. "I'm immortal. Were you actually afraid for me?"

Sybil gave a tiny shrug. "Maybe you're immortal, but I think you can still bleed. You put your body between mine and an attack. Yes, I was worried for you."

Kadar let out a startled laugh behind her. "She was. She was worried about all of us."

She turned her head to scowl at him. "Quit laughing. Any of you might have gotten hurt. It would have been my fault."

"She's a darling," the dragon said, shaking his head. "Take her away before I have to pound myself into her again."

"She's going to be far too busy for that." Abaran's eyes glittered with lust. He scooped her up and slung her naked body over his shoulder, her bare butt thrust up. He rubbed the palm of one hand over the rounded globes as he carried her off.

The bold, openly sexual caress made her shiver. For the time being, she was his. And he was planning to take her every way possible.

Her nipples felt hard and tight against his back. His muscles felt rigid and ungiving, muscles as hard as steel covered with leather. He was like a walking fetish, she thought, feeling dizzy. If the touch of leather against naked skin did it for her, she'd be his slave.

It was impossible to pay attention to anything but the way

he held her, the way their bodies brushed as he moved with long, rapid strides. The smoky scent of him. The visceral memory of his wickedly curved flesh burying itself inside her. The knowledge that for the next twenty-four hours she was in his power, both thrilled and terrified her.

If it was this difficult to be alone with a demon, how hard was it going to be to put herself into the hands of a fae who got off on pain?

Abaran lowered her down onto a soft bed, and Sybil blinked as she realized they'd already arrived at their destination. She managed to tear her eyes away from the sight of Abaran stripping off his pants to look around.

The walls were covered with thick vines that held large, waxy blossoms. The floor looked like it was carpeted with springy moss. The bed he'd placed her on was made of dark, carved wood with a deep mattress and covered with what felt like silk.

"Is it night?" Sybil asked, her throat hoarse from tension.

"Yes." Abaran stood over her, fully naked. "Look up."

She did, and saw an expanse of stars overhead. The room appeared to be open to the sky. "The flowers are real? Night blooming?"

"Yes." He put his hands on her knees and pushed them apart so he could kneel between them.

Sybil shivered as he loomed over her. Then he lowered

himself down to cover her body with his. The sensation of being blanketed with hot flesh the texture of leather would probably never lose its novelty, she thought, and wondered if the demon would be settling on top of her often enough for her to test that theory.

Impossible to guess.

"Are you cold?" Abaran's voice was unexpectedly gentle.

"Nervous." She placed her hands on his shoulders, not sure if he wanted her to touch him or how. "Trying to adjust to a steady stream of strange men in bed with me."

He let out a laugh, a low, dark sound that sent frissons of alarm down her spine. "There are only five of us."

"Only." Sybil echoed the word with irony and turned her face so that her lips brushed his cheek. The texture pleased her, seduced her into extending the gesture without thinking.

Abaran let out a fierce, hungry sound that made her freeze. Then his mouth found hers and branded her lips with a searing kiss. His tongue demanded entry, thrust into her mouth, rubbed against her tongue. His body rocked on hers, pushed her thighs wider apart as he settled himself into the cradle of her hips. Then without warning, he tore his mouth from hers and rose up.

"Turn over. If I stay on you like that another second, I'll be inside you. And I want to touch you first."

His guttural command made her tremble, but she rolled

over onto her belly. Her butt tightened in nervous reaction when he ran his hand over it.

"Did the wolf take you here?" Abaran's fingertips traced the valley between her buttocks. The soft skin there reacted pleasurably to his touch.

"No."

"No? Did the dragon put something larger than the point of his tail into this?" The pad of Abaran's finger pressed against her anus, stroked, caressed the sensitive tissue and coaxed a response from her.

"No," she breathed out.

"No." Abaran pushed the tip of his finger into the entry Kadar had oiled so carefully. The slick lubricant eased his way, allowing him to push deeper. "Why not?" He pushed a second finger in to join the first, stretching her almost painfully despite Kenric's similar treatment of her and Kadar's erotic play.

"Too tight," Sybil managed to say as her body struggled to adjust to the unfamiliar invasion. Abaran began to push a third finger into her and she moaned, twisting away.

"Too tight." Abaran's other hand found her hip, imprisoned her, held her down while he worked the third finger deeper. "Too tight to take a cock? Too tight to take this?" He pushed harder and she moaned again at the sensual invasion that made her want to pull away and at the same time made her want to arch her lower back to invite more.

"Yes." Her voice sounded throaty, aroused. She bit her lip as he fingered her into a state of unaccustomed pleasure.

"Ah, so hot, so tight." He pulled his digits free one at a time, then gently caressed the rosy opening he'd plundered. "So ready."

"So not. I've never." She swallowed convulsively at the thought of how easily he could guide himself into place and press forward, working himself inside that tight hole.

"We'll change that soon." His whisper shivered over her skin, fierce and exultant. "Right now, I'm going to make you come for me."

Abaran covered her body with his and pushed his legs between hers. He slid his other hand underneath her to cup her mound in his leathery palm. His fingertips pressed into her sex, not quite penetrating her. The rounded swells of her butt cushioned the thick length of his penis. He rocked his hips to stroke himself along the crease that separated the twin globes as he worked two fingers between her folds, opening her, entering her while his palm massaged her clit.

"Oh," Sybil whispered and arched her pelvis into his hand. "Abaran, that feels so good."

"Not as good as it's going to feel when it's my cock between your legs."

His words made heat coil low in her belly. Abaran worked a third finger inside her sheath, giving her more, while the tantalizing memory of his wickedly curved flesh driving into her, made her shudder with yearning.

His shaft glided along the soft curves of her ass in time with the movements of his hand. Desire built and rapidly grew into need. The rhythm of his fingers pushing into her had her gasping, shuddering, struggling for something out of reach. He felt the rising tension in her body and sped up, twisting his fingers in her sheath while he ground his palm against her clit. Sybil nearly came up off the bed, keening, her body convulsing as she orgasmed.

She collapsed under him, quiescent and trembling with aftershocks while he pumped himself between her buttocks, coming with a hoarse shout. Heated liquid spilled along the base of her spine and the curves of her ass. Abaran continued to thrust against her, rubbing the slick ejaculate into her skin.

He nuzzled the back of her neck and squeezed her mound as he slowly withdrew his fingers. "Sweet," Abaran murmured, kissing the curve of her shoulder.

Sybil let out a soft laugh. "Sweet? You just came all over my ass."

"And you just came in my hand." He pulled it out from under her and moved to her side, touching her in leisurely exploration.

Abaran searched out the sensitive points along her spine, the backs of her legs, the delicate bones of her ankles. He caressed her arms and her ribs, then rolled her onto her back to stroke her belly, her throat, the sensitive undersides of her breasts, the nipples that drew taut at his touch.

His hands on her sent tingles of awareness and shivers of delight dancing over her skin. She might be conflicted about it, but she couldn't deny that her body hungered for his touch. She wanted more of him. The slide of silk under her and the rough sensation of leather where his body brushed hers thrilled her.

"Sweet witch," Aharan breathed, taking her mouth again. Her lips parted to invite his tongue to slide inside and twine with hers. The dark taste of him intoxicated her and the gentle stroke of his hand on her hair soothed her. "I'm glad I took you away. I don't want to share this first time with another male."

"Does that mean you don't want to do a threesome anymore?" Sybil asked.

"No." He cupped a hand over her breast and squeezed lightly. "I want to share you after I've marked you. I'd love to be deep in your sweet ass while you come with another man's shaft planted in you all the way to your womb."

Sybil could see the attraction for her, but not for him. "Why?"

"Because it will be ecstasy for you, and that will heighten the pleasure you give both of your partners." He pinched her nipple, then lightly stroked the underside of her breast, raising gooseflesh with the contrast of rough and gentle. "Because I want to see you take more pleasure than you think you can stand. Because it will make you even tighter and I want to feel your flesh squeezing me so hard I can't hold back."

"Oh." She rested her hand on his chest, exploring his hard, leathery muscles with tiny movements. "I didn't think it would feel better to the man. I always thought it was a purely female fantasy."

"It also scares you," Abaran said. "I want you to do something with me that scares you. You let the dragon ride you while I watched, and let him watch while I gave your body a taste of mine. I want you to spread your thighs for another man while I pleasure myself in your hot ass because I command it."

She leaned her head against his shoulder because his words made her dizzy, even laying down. "You get off on fear?"

"It's not about fear." He stroked her hair with gentle fingers. "It's about your surrender."

"I'm alone and naked with a demon. I'm still scared about that," Sybil muttered.

"Scared you'll grow to like it?" Abaran's knowing voice mingled with the scent and feel of his body and she felt her inner muscles tighten in reaction.

"Not exactly." She was afraid she already did. She'd loved kneeling in submission while Kenric took her from behind with animalistic lust. She'd loved being chained and displayed for Kadar, and the exhibitionist thrill she'd never imagined feeling. She'd loved the intensity of orgasm Kadar had given her by driving into her while Abaran watched.

"No? What do you fear, then?"

She rubbed her cheek against his. "I'm afraid I'll crave all of you after this is over."

"Like a drug," Abaran mused. "First one's free and then you're hooked."

Sybil nodded. "Something like that."

His penis hardened perceptively, swelling thicker, lengthening. "That pleases me."

"I thought Ronan was the sadist."

"I think I want to feed your addiction."

Heat flared over her skin. She drew in a sharp breath and fought to control it. "Abaran."

"I feel it." He stroked her from breast to hip, almost seeming to luxuriate in her escalated body temperature. His touch made it worse, as if the demonic power inside her sought to ground itself in demon flesh. The fever abruptly shot higher and flames burst out, engulfing her from head to toe.

"You're on fire for me," Abaran murmured, sliding his tongue between her lips while she shuddered and burned and drank in his exotic flavor.

When he freed her mouth, she gasped out, "You're making it worse."

"I'm going to make it so much better." He drew back and she blinked at what looked like wings unfurled from his shoulders. He lowered himself onto his back beside her and put his hands on her waist, lifting her onto him. When he had her on top, he put one hand on her butt, the other on the lower curve of her spine and pressed her body into his as if he was absorbing the heat she gave off. Wings closed around her and cocooned them together.

"Now I make you mine," Abaran said in a thick voice.

The heat was unbearable. Sybil tried to pull away and found herself held prisoner by his hands and the leathery wings that folded tightly around her, smothering the flames. "Let me go."

"You need me." The demon's hands gripped her hips, lifted her enough to find his angle. The mark on her breast thrummed and magic gathered in the air. Abaran pulled her down and simultaneously pushed up into her. His entry was rough and rapid, and it made her groan in unwanted pleasure as her body adjusted to his.

"I don't want to need you." Sybil fought the urge to ride him, to press her legs wider apart and take him deeper.

"Maybe we don't want to need you, either." He found her mouth and his teeth grazed her lower lip, a sharp pain he immediately made her forget with the erotic slide of his tongue along hers.

She was burning. She was melting. She dissolved against him, fed the heat inside her into his kiss, and succumbed to the raw need for his hard length driving between her legs. The inescapable grip of his fingers as they dug into her ass and held her immobile while he thrust up into her thrilled her.

Her breasts were crushed against his chest, her pelvis cradled by his while he pistoned into her. Her breath came in ragged pants as the flames banked.

"There," Abaran breathed against her lips. "One fire out, and another to quench."

They rocked together, bodies locked and straining for release. He brought her to the edge and pushed her over, making her spine bow and her body draw taut in orgasm before he let himself join her, spilling himself into her in a liquid rush while a burst of magic released.

twelve

When Abaran's wings opened a long time later, Sybil rested with her cheek on his shoulder, her torso pressed to his, her thighs draped over his, and tightened herself around the circumference of his shaft still planted deep inside her.

"Addicted yet?" Abaran stroked the curve of her bare butt with one hand. His other arm clamped her body against his.

"Maybe." She didn't have another explanation for her abandoned response to three different men. Not that they were in any way interchangeable.

"How does the mark feel?"

She exhaled in a huff, blowing a stray curl away from her eye. "Fine now. It sort of burns when it happens."

"That would explain the way you jerked and screamed when you came."

"No, that was from the cattle prod you call a penis."

Abaran laughed, a low, dark sound of masculine satisfaction. "You like it."

"Apparently there isn't anything I don't like. I like submissive sex, voyeuristic sex, exhibitionist sex, and sex with a series of changing partners. Who knew?" Her flippant tone disguised the tight pressure in her throat.

Abaran squeezed her ass. "Wait until Ronan gets his hands on you."

She shuddered. "I wish that wolf had just killed me."

"You don't mean that."

"No, I don't mean that. But I don't know how to cope with this, either."

"I thought you were coping very well." He rolled with her, coming to rest on top of her, still pressing deep inside. His penis pulsed as if heavy with need.

"Again?" Sybil asked the question in disbelief. But she couldn't stop herself from wrapping her arms and legs around him and arching up under him. She felt the same need, as if her body was attuned to his. It wasn't the shattering intensity of desire she felt for Kenric, or the cheerful lust she shared with Kadar. More like the pull of twin magnets.

"I don't want you to suffer by making you wait too long for your next fix."

"How generous," Sybil said in a tone that clearly conveyed the opposite thought even as her inner muscles tightened eagerly around him.

"Try not to set the bed on fire," Abaran suggested, and began to move inside her.

sybil woke up alone, feeling pleasantly relaxed and a little hung over. When she stretched and rolled over on her stomach, raw silk caressed her naked skin.

She felt amazingly safe considering she was in a demon's bed. Safety was a concept she clearly didn't grasp. She drummed her fingers on the sheet and thought about Kadar's conclusion that she'd spent her whole life in danger until now. She'd thought her life had been perfectly safe until she followed an impulse and found her life exploding in dust and splinters along with her apartment door. If he was right, her view of the world was upside down.

Her coven hadn't been trying to keep her from blowing the rule of three to smithereens. They'd been fishing for demon magic and keeping her ignorant so she'd make the best bait.

"So who do you trust?" Sybil asked out loud. The group of wise women she'd known all her life? Or the five men who were seducing her, body and soul?

Whether she wanted to or not, Sybil needed all five of them. Abaran had said they didn't want to need her, either.

Understandable, given what happened the last time they'd allied with a witch.

"Enough of this." Annoyed by her thoughts, Sybil jumped up and padded outside, naked and barefoot. Since she hadn't been paying attention to the route Abaran took when he carried her off, she had no idea where she was. But she could hear the river, so she followed the sound until she found her way to an overlook above it.

Could witches really fly? Water was a good thing to have under her while she tried to find out. Sybil eyed the distance and decided she'd just get wet if the answer was no.

She balanced on the balls of her feet as she looked down at the river. No wings. Broomsticks were too ridiculous to consider.

"Levitate," Sybil said out loud. And what spell would do that? Even if she knew, did she dare try when she might say the wrong words out loud with horrifying consequences? No spells. Which left . . .

She closed her eyes and called prickling heat to the palms of her hands. A burning sensation spread over her arms, down her body. She felt her hair stirring in a wind that hadn't been there a moment before. Then flames clothed her. It didn't hurt, maybe because she wasn't fighting it. Or maybe because having three-fifths of the star tattoo had shifted her internal balance of power. The necklace Kadar had given her seemed to be helping, too, singing to the fire she'd called.

She concentrated on letting the power rise, carrying her with it. When she opened her eyes, her feet were floating off the ground. She laughed, exultant and disbelieving at the same time, and spread her arms wide, leaning toward the river. Then the flames winked out and she dropped like a rock through the empty air.

Abaran was waiting on the bank when she finished washing. "Enjoy your swim?"

"Yes, thanks." Sybil sluiced water from her naked body and joined him on dry land. "Did you bring a towel?"

"You didn't bring one? What did you do, fall in the river?"

"Yes."

The dark demon grinned. Then laughed.

Sybil aimed her palms at him, gathered power, and shoved it in his direction. Abaran slid back from the force. He planted his feet and raised his hands in mock surrender. "That's new. Been practicing?"

"Yep. And for a minute there, I flew over the water."

"Show me."

She focused and called the fire. It lifted her a few inches above the ground. Then the flames banked and she landed again with a thump. "I keep getting more control as I get more of the mark. And this helps." She touched the necklace.

"Good." His expression turned serious. "You're going to need all the help you can get."

"Against the bad guys? Or so I don't turn into one of them?"

"Both."

Sybil wrapped her arms around herself, suddenly chilled. "Abaran, you're the expert on demons. Tell me about the ones that attacked. What do they do? How do you fight them?"

He took hold of her shoulder and turned her toward a path that led back up to his retreat. "Tempter demons. They attack where they find an opening," he answered as they began the climb. "They'll use your own weaknesses against you. Right now, your lack of control is a weakness that invites a stronger force to invade."

"So the best offense is a good defense?"

"It's a start."

Sybil reached the top of the path and paused to look down

at the river. "Yeah, but which one is more helpful in an enemy encounter?"

"That depends. If you find yourself in enemy hands, you use whatever techniques, tactics, and weapons you possess. Whatever will give you the greatest chance of success and survival." Abaran put a hand to the small of her back. "You should stay inside where you're harder to sense. Especially when you're playing with power they can home in on."

"Right." Sybil got moving. "Can you home in on it?"

"How do you think I found you?"

She stopped in her tracks and turned to face him. "Does it draw you?"

"I don't want it for myself, if that's what you mean." Abaran brushed a hand along her bare upper arm. The contact made her shiver. His midnight eyes deepened. "But touching you is the closest thing to the touch of my kind I've felt in centuries."

She blinked. "I feel like a demon to you?"

"There's a resonance. A power signature, if you like."

That explained the magnetic pull she felt when they touched. "Huh."

"We shouldn't stay out here." He caught her hand and drew her under cover. "You're still too vulnerable."

"And you're not? Even Superman had kryptonite."

"I'm not a fledgling."

Sybil frowned. "But you're a demon. And you sided against them. They have to hate you for that."

His teeth flashed in a fierce smile. "I'm not a tempter demon, and I'm in full command of my powers."

She meant to ask what sort of demon he was, but he settled his hands on her waist and drew her closer until their bodies brushed. The swell of his curved penis brushed her belly.

"Hey." Sybil tipped her head up to frown at him. "Don't think you can just put your hands on me and distract . . . oh." Her voice cut off as he lifted her up against his torso and cupped her bare ass in his hands.

"Wrap your legs around me."

She did, winding arms and legs around him to keep from falling. He walked her back to the bed, lowered her onto it and followed her down to cover her body with his. He rubbed his leathery skin against hers, making her nipples tighten. His weight filled her with a thrum of sensual anticipation.

"Company's on the way."

"Kadar?"

Abaran's penis nudged between her legs. "No." He rubbed the head of his cock along her folds. Her body reacted to the intimate contact, her sex already softening and growing slicker.

Abaran's tongue twined with hers as he slowly pushed all the way inside and she opened to take him. His body rocked into hers again and again, insistent, seductive, demanding, until she was on the verge of orgasm. Then he pulled all the way out, leaving her aroused and trembling.

"So cruel," she muttered.

Abaran's face turned knowing. "Tell me that after I make you the center in your first threesome."

"Did you start without me?"

Sybil turned her face toward the sound of Kenric's voice, caught by a surge of hunger for the sight of his face. She met his gaze and forgot to breathe when she saw raw desire in his golden gaze. She couldn't look away. An almost painful yearning swept through her. Not for sex, although she could almost feel every cell in her body straining toward him. For something deeper, more primal and wordless.

Kenric took in the sight of Sybil sprawled under Abaran, the scent of her arousal thick in the air, and felt his cock twitch in reaction. She looked sensual and abandoned, her eyes heavy with pleasure, her cheeks flushed, her parted legs and glistening sex an invitation he intended to accept.

Her hair, a tangle of streaked shades of sun and sand, spilled across the silk sheet beneath her. He wanted to touch it, to see if it felt as soft as he remembered. He wanted to touch her skin and feel the slide of warm, living silk under his hands instead of the phantom touch that had haunted him for two nights. He wanted to fit his hands over her breasts and rasp his palms against the tight buds of her nipples and hear her breath catch. He wanted to claim her mouth and drink in the passionate cries still echoing in his mind.

He wanted her.

For two days and nights, the sound and scent of her had remained with him, compelling him. He'd nearly sought her out a dozen times. If she was a wolf, he'd think they'd mated. But she wasn't a wolf, despite the way his cock knotted to lock their bodies together every time he entered her.

His desire should have eased after he'd given her the mark and sated himself with her. But it seemed the more he had of her, the more he hungered, as if she fed an appetite that could never be appeased.

It had overtaken him the first time he'd touched her at the oasis, when he'd lost his head and brought her to the peak with his mouth instead of his hands. Because touching her wasn't enough. He'd needed to know the taste of her.

After marking her, he'd taken her to Kadar, and bound her in chains, still wanting her. He hadn't been able to resist touching her while she was shackled and spread wide for pleasure. He'd left her there and taken his hand to his aching shaft while he imagined standing between her open legs and driving into her willing body.

Now he stood beside Abaran's bed, watching as Abaran

guided his shaft toward her ready entry, pressed home, and worked his hips in a lazy in and out motion.

Watching another man on top of her aroused Kenric. It made him want to compete, to prove himself the alpha male, the one who could lavish the most pleasure on a female. It also stirred some feeling he couldn't name, a desire to see her experience a depth of satisfaction beyond anything she'd ever known.

Abaran stroked in and out of her again. She moved with him, her eyes half-closing in obvious enjoyment. The sight made Kenric feel tender, indulgent. It also made him feel fierce and dominant. He wanted to cherish her sexual response. He wanted to drive into her with relentless savagery.

He joined them on the mattress and stretched alongside the pair, giving in to the temptation to toy with her hair. Soft strands slid through his fingers. He tightened his hand around the silk of her hair, holding on instead of allowing it to spill away from him.

Her scent filled his nostrils. Aroused woman, overlaid with a heady wash of magic and a clean, herbal fragrance.

His thick shaft jerked as if she'd reached out and touched him. He used the fistful of her hair to tug her head toward his. Her eyes met his, a deep blue he could lose himself in. Her lips parted as if inviting his kiss.

He held back with an effort of will.

A witch had betrayed him and that had been the end and the beginning. A book of demon magic had slipped out of his grasp, possibly drawn away by a spell she'd left waiting in the event of her untimely death.

Now the damned book was back, with another witch. He wouldn't let it go astray again. He wouldn't let this witch betray them all this time. She wouldn't get the opportunity. He knew better than to trust her.

Trust wasn't required for what he wanted from her.

He pressed his forefinger between her parted lips and watched as she closed them around his digit, licking at the pad of his finger as he pushed it into her mouth. Her body arched under Abaran's.

Kenric wanted her soft, slender body arching up under his, writhing in ecstatic need. He wanted to bury his cock in her slick heat, to feel her inner walls squeezing his shaft and her hard little nipples rubbing against his chest as he moved on top of her.

"Ready to be taken by two men at once?" Kenric stroked his finger in and out of her mouth in a graphic demonstration of the way he intended to use her body.

Her eyes darkened and she sucked his finger hard.

"I'll take that as a yes."

Thirteen

Sybil tasted salt and a hint of musk as she drew Kenric's finger into her mouth. Wolf, she thought, almost giddy at the thought of the great beast he could become. He was wolf-like as a man, dominant and watchful and predatory. He was looking at her now as if she was something he'd run to ground and was preparing to pounce on.

Being the focus of that look heightened her awareness of Abaran's body on hers, in hers. It added a layer of eroticism to the experience. Not just because she was watched. Because she was watched by Kenric. She'd knew she'd feel differently if it was Kadar who'd joined them, and that difference was impossible to ignore.

He slid his finger out of her lips and traced a line down her throat to the valley between her breasts, touching the pendant that nestled there. He frowned. "What is that?"

She gave him a lazy, satisfied grin to cover the emotion his touch stirred. "Kadar was feeling appreciative."

Something flickered in his gold eyes. "Kadar doesn't part with his treasures."

She moved one bare shoulder in a small shrug. "Maybe he figures it's still his property and I'm a roving display."

Abaran let out a soft laugh at that. "You are roving."

She stuck her tongue out at the demon. He bent his head to suck it into his mouth, replacing the musk of wolf on her tongue with the dark, smoky flavor of demon. No, she realized a beat later, not replacing. Mingling, so that she tasted both of them together.

Abaran let her tongue slide free and then touched the tip of his to hers before he spoke again, this time to Kenric. "The dragon has a fondness for our little witch. He may even be besotted with her."

"Then why is he not here?" Kenric released her hair and moved his hand down the curve of her neck to the sensitive hollows of her throat. "She expected him."

"When I went to get him, he was busy studying something. He said I should invite you in his place."

Sybil frowned, wondering what Kadar was studying and if it had anything to do with her own questions about the coven. "Did he say what?"

Abaran planted his palms on the mattress and levered himself up, driving himself deeper in the process. The pressure and stimulation focused her attention on the present. "Why so curious about another male when you have two of us to entertain?"

She breathed out a sigh, rocking her hips under his to take more. "You are entertaining. Especially when you do that. I'm sorry I pushed you around earlier."

Abaran stroked out, in, then all the way out, withdrawing from her and kneeling between her sprawled legs with his erect penis jutting up. "Kitten has claws."

"She pushed you around?" Kenric asked. He gave the two of them a measuring look.

"She did. She's not up to my weight, but she's getting better," the demon replied. "Stronger, more in control." He gave one bare nipple a tug that made Sybil's inner muscles clench in reaction. "Show the wolf your new trick."

She raised a brow at his choice of words. "Am I a kitten or a puppy now?"

"Since I intend to make you sit up and beg, draw your own

conclusions." Abaran waited, daring her to perform with his eyes.

Fine. Great. Perform on command for an audience. No pressure. Sybil closed her eyes and let magic burn. Now that she had the hang of it, it was easier than trying to stuff it down. She focused on the silk sheet under her and then pushed it away with her will. When she opened her eyes, she floated just above the mattress, reclined on her back. "Ta da."

Then the fire damped and she landed with a bounce.

"Impressive." Kenric's face was unreadable, his tone flat.

"Not to you." She rolled onto her side, propped herself up on an elbow, and trailed her fingers down his chest, following the arrow of body hair that led to his penis. "You only have one use for a witch."

"How did you do that?"

"No clue."

"And what gave you the idea to try it?" Kenric settled a hand on her breast, stroking her as he spoke.

"Kadar said I could fly. I thought he was yanking my chain, but then I figured why not see?"

"The dragon told you to jump off a cliff, so you did?" Amusement rang in Abaran's voice.

"Shut up." Sybil raised one foot to poke the demon's belly with her toe.

"Give me something better to do with my mouth," he suggested.

His mouth would torment her no matter what he did with it, but the thought of having it between her legs made her muscles turn to liquid. She lowered her foot, placed both of her soles flat against the mattress, settled onto her back and spread her thighs wide apart in silent invitation.

The demon lowered his head to kiss her belly.

"Lower," Sybil said, her breath catching at the thought of Abaran's tongue sliding between her folds while Kenric watched. Kenric's hand moved on her breast, kneading her flesh, making her ache for more.

"You smell like sex," Abaran said in a dark, hungry voice. "Delicious."

"You sound like night," she answered. "All shadows and secret dreams."

"And your secret dream is to surrender to the dark." Abaran touched the tip of his tongue to her exposed flesh. The tiniest contact, but it made her shiver.

She closed her eyes and surrendered to her demon lover as his lips brushed the bud of her clitoris in a soft kiss. Then lower. She arched in response as his lips opened and his tongue thrust into her core, the movement lifting her ribcage and pushing her breasts up like an offering.

Kenric's mouth closed over the aureole of one swollen

crest while his hand tightened on the other in a light squeeze. Two pairs of warm lips suckled her sex and her nipple at the same time. The reality of it undid her. She'd had a taste of two men touching her together, and now she was going to have a banquet.

Abaran tasted her deeply, thoroughly, repeatedly, licking inside her, laving her folds and her clit with his tongue, applying light suction with his mouth. Her womb clenched and her hips moved restlessly, unable to remain still.

Kenric turned his attention from one breast to the other, dragging his tongue across her curves before closing on her again. She dug her hands into his hair and urged him on. Her head fell back, leaving the column of her throat exposed. His lips moved up to explore that vulnerability. He kissed her softly, then raked the upper curves of her breasts with his teeth.

Abaran gripped her hips and thrust his tongue into her again and again. The penetration made her wild for more. When she trembled on the brink of orgasm, he raised his head and left her wanting.

"Ready to beg?"

"Yes. Dammit."

Abaran laughed at her answer and moved to stretch out beside her. He cupped a hand over her sex and rubbed in a circle, giving her enough pressure to keep her on the edge but not enough to let her go over it. "Beg me to let you come."

She turned her head to touch her lips to his, tasting herself on him. "Please," she said, her voice husky with desire.

"In time. First, pleasure the wolf with your mouth and tongue until he wants to sink himself between your legs instead of between your lips."

The two of them were going to drive her crazy. Sybil nodded her assent. Kenric rose up over her, lowering himself until the head of his penis brushed her mouth. She parted her lips to welcome him and brushed her tongue along his shaft, savoring the taste of him.

Abaran's hands stroked her torso and made her nerve endings sing with his touch. Smoke and musk, demon and wolf. They went to her head and left her giddy and breathless. Her lips circled Kenric's rigid flesh as she opened wide to take him as deep as she could. Her body moved under Abaran's hands, delighted by his touch. Two lovers, so different, so close. Their nearness made her hunger for more. It wasn't enough. She wanted them closer. She ached to be pressed between them, pierced by both of them.

Abaran's hand smoothed over her belly and down to cup her sex again, and she rocked her hips up into the caress. He pressed his fingertips against her core. The shallow penetration made her groan and suck Kenric harder. When he pulled out of her mouth, her eyes fluttered open. She watched him watching her as Abaran's fingers pushed into her, slid out, then in again, coating them. Then Abaran spread her own lubrication over her anus, and worked two fingers into her, then scissored them, opening her. And she knew this time he intended to go further.

She relaxed and arched the small of her back, pushing back to take more, knowing she could trust him to give her only pleasure.

Kenric moved onto his back and reached for her. She straddled him and made a low sound of satisfaction when her sex pressed against his thick length. It felt so good to have her body pressed against his. Right.

Abaran came behind her, covered her back with his torso, and brushed a tender kiss against the nape of her neck.

Kenric gripped her hips and lifted her up until her core was aligned with his shaft. Then he pulled her down and pushed up into her, filling her. While she adjusted to the length and width of him deep inside her, Abaran began to thrust himself into her from behind. Sybil groaned at the sensation of being penetrated in two places at once, the intensity of it paralyzing her.

Abaran gave her inch after inch of his hard shaft until he'd worked himself all the way into her anal passage and she was stretched impossibly tight. Kenric's penis swelled inside her as the knot formed, and the additional stimulation made her inner muscles quiver in a precursor to orgasm.

"Now, little witch," Abaran breathed near her ear. "We're going to fuck you so well, you'll come from the memory of it a year from now."

The heat of Kenric's body under hers contrasted with the leathery feel of Abaran's skin above her. Their mingled scents made her head spin. The two men began to move as if choreographed, one sliding out, the other pressing deep in a counter stroke to each other. One of them always filling her completely with his length, the other's thickness at her entry stretching her to the limit.

Then they both thrust into her together, their joint possession of her body almost more than she could contain. She struggled to accommodate both of them all the way inside her, as deep as they could go, and heard herself keening from the exquisite torment.

They took her together with relentless thoroughness, driving deep, giving her all she could take and then more than she thought she could. She broke first, spine bowing from the force of her orgasm as she came in endless waves of ecstasy. Abaran followed, spending himself with a fierce shout as he tunneled into her.

He was still thick and hard and buried deep in her ass, heightening her pleasure, when Kenric began to drive into her hard and fast. He ejaculated into her with each furious stroke, and the hot liquid sensation deep in her core sent her off again, her inner muscles squeezing the two cocks inside her so the pleasure was shared by all three of them.

Afterward, she rested on Kenric's chest, listening to his heart pound and wondering if hers was racing too or if it had stopped. She felt light and unreal. Kenric's body supported her from beneath, strong and solid. Abaran's body curved over hers from above, protective and plundering at the same time.

She wanted to stay that way as long as possible, connected to both of them, possessed, ravished.

Abaran slowly withdrew from her tight rear entrance and stretched out beside her. He kissed her, long and sweet, while little tremors of pleasure rippled through her inner muscles clenched around Kenric's shaft. When the knot released and Kenric lifted her up and off, she wanted to protest.

The two of them lowered her to the mattress, turning her onto her back. She shivered, feeling cold and empty. Then the two of them pressed close on either side of her, facing each other on their sides, hands caressing her. She closed her eyes and absorbed their warmth.

"Were we too much for you, witch?" Abaran asked, his voice dark and knowing.

She wanted to say something flippant and light, but her throat was tight and she had no words. So she shook her head once in silence, keeping her eyes closed.

She wanted Kenric to kiss her, but it was Abaran who did,

covering her mouth with his and licking at the seam of her lips until she opened for him. His hand searched out her nipple and rolled it between his fingers as his tongue thrust inside to mate with hers. She kissed him back, helpless to do anything else. The taste of him was a pleasure all its own and she opened wider to deepen the kiss.

The mattress shifted and her right side cooled when Kenric stood. She opened her eyes to watch him go, wishing she could ask him to stay. He paused in the doorframe and looked back at her. His eyes caught hers. She met his gaze, unblinking, as she parted her thighs, took Abaran's hand and guided it between them. Hunger and satisfaction gleamed in Kenric's amber depths, as if he wanted to touch her there and found satiation by proxy. Then she let her lashes drift down as Abaran's fingers pushed into her core. When she raised them again, Kenric was gone.

"Nervous?"

"Yes." Sybil admitted. She slowed her pace and her breathing deliberately, trying to fake her way to calm.

"You know I have to give you to Adrian. And Adrian, in turn, has to give you to Ronan. You need to complete the mark's transfer."

Abaran sounded so calm and reasonable. Sybil wished she shared his assurance.

"Something bad is going to happen," she muttered, feeling the invisible press of some nameless dread. Her skin prickled. Between her breasts, the necklace felt hot. She glanced down at it and saw it giving off a reddish glow that reinforced the sense of warning.

"Nothing bad will happen. You'll be deprived of my body, but Adrian will fuck you nearly as well as I do."

She shook her head. "I'm not nervous about Adrian. If I can handle a demon, I can survive a night with a vampire."

Abaran gave her a sidelong look. "Did it bother you that Kenric knotted you when the three of us were together?"

"No, I'm used to that. I like it," she admitted, feeling deviant.

"You mean that's not the only time?"

Sybil felt herself blushing. "No, every time. And how could you tell, anyway?"

"When we had you double penetrated, there was only a thin membrane between us. I felt everything you felt."

"Oh." She blinked. "I didn't realize. That must feel . . . interesting."

"Very. But what's more interesting is that Kenric does lupine lust with you."

"He told me it wasn't supposed to happen, but I'm kind of a walking anomaly. Witch powered by demon sealed by goddess with a garnish of magic fairy necklace. Weird happenings are becoming my new normal."

"And that's all he told you?" Abaran's midnight eyes searched hers. "That it wasn't supposed to happen?"

"What else was there to say?"

"Maybe you should ask him that."

"I'll put it on my to-do list." She pushed it aside for the moment. Now was not the time to think about her confusing relationship with the werewolf. If it could be called a relationship. "Meanwhile, I think my Spidey sense is telling me something."

"Your Spidey sense?" Abaran raised a brow at her choice of words, but he stopped and did a slow turn, looking in all directions. She got the feeling he was using more than his eyes to scan. "I sense nothing."

The red glow from the stone she wore centered on his chest. It looked like a laser sight targeting him. Dread pooled in her abdomen. "Be careful after you leave me, Abaran. Promise me you'll be careful."

"I'm immortal," Abaran assured her, amusement clear in his voice. "Don't worry about me. You should worry about yourself. I've seen what women look like when Adrian's done with them."

She spread her hand over the tattoo outlined starkly on his

bare skin. "You might be immortal, but you can still bleed. Promise to be careful. Please."

"I've damaged your brain with pleasure," the demon mused out loud. "My naked glory was too much for your delicate sensibilities and your mind has broken from the strain."

"Probably." She caressed him, memorizing the leathery texture of his skin, then burrowed close to breathe in his smoky scent. "Since you've destroyed me with sex, humor me. It's the least you can do."

"Careful, witch, I might come to think you truly care."

Her throat ached and she hugged him tighter. "If anything happened to you, I'd pine."

"That would be a tragedy." Abaran cupped her ass in both hands and squeezed. "All right, witch. I promise to be careful."

His promise didn't reassure her. But it was the best she could hope for. "Thank you."

"Adrian will keep you too busy to miss me."

Her lips brushed his throat. "I miss you already."

fourteen

While Abaran knocked on the vampire's door, Sybil shifted nervously from one foot to the other. "Does he sleep in a coffin? Is there some sort of Renfield on duty?"

He turned to stare at her. "Did you hit your head when you fell in the river?"

She stuck her tongue out at him.

The door opened on silent hinges, and Adrian stood there, broad and solid, regarding both of them with an unfathomable expression. There was a suggestion of military discipline in his stance. Sybil stopped fidgeting and tried to stand straight. It was far too late to wish for a good hair day, but she could try for good posture.

"Hi. Um, remember me? Well, it's your night to have supernatural sex with me." She smiled brightly and added, "I'm A negative. I hope that isn't a problem for you."

Abaran looked at Adrian and shrugged. He extended his wings and furled them around her, cocooning her body against his. His lips brushed her hair as he spoke. "I will return in twenty-four hours to escort you to Ronan." He released her, retracting his wings and folding them invisibly into his back. He put his hands on her shoulders and pushed her at Adrian.

"Now go and torment the vampire. He can count the hours until I take your troublesome person off his hands."

Sybil walked past Adrian, who held the door open for her without a word. It closed behind her with a whisper. She wrapped her arms around herself to ward off the chill that descended on her.

A moment later, Adrian broke the silence. "What are you wearing?"

Sybil glanced down at the diamond that caught all available light in a rainbow of color and shimmered against her skin. The warning red was gone. "A necklace."

"I recognize that stone. I last saw it in a dragon's hoard."

"I know." She touched it, feeling almost as if it gave her a way to touch Kadar. It was so like him, larger than life and breathtaking. "He's very generous."

"That isn't the word one usually uses to describe a dragon. And Abaran wrapped you in his wings. What of the wolf?"

"I don't want to talk about the wolf." Sybil huddled into herself, feeling small and cold. "He hates me. No, that's not true. He'd have to care to hate me. I'm too insignificant for him to hate."

"Insignificant?" The vampire moved closer to her. "Why do I smell him on your skin? The scent only lingers a few hours and you haven't been his for the past two nights."

"He was with us. Earlier." Sybil made a gesture back toward the door, indicating the direction she'd last seen Abaran. "Abaran wanted a threesome."

"And the wolf who finds you insignificant volunteered?"

She shrugged. "Probably everybody else was busy. What's your point?"

"The wolf had no reason to be with you after he marked you unless it was for his own pleasure." Adrian shook his head. "I wouldn't have believed it possible. You've bewitched them."

Her lips moved soundlessly, shaping the word. Bewitched? Was it true? Was the power inside her working against the men who were trying to help her?

"I didn't mean to," she said in a voice thick with unshed tears. "How can I undo it?"

"I'll study the matter." The vampire made a gesture of invitation that struck her as aristocratic. "In the meantime, I'll leave you to rest. You'll find a room ready for you through there."

Sybil nodded and went with dragging feet. The room was beautiful. The bed was soft. She pulled a linen sheet and a blanket over herself and admired the fine weave and artistic pattern. Adrian had excellent taste. The style of his house reminded her of a Roman villa, and she wondered if he had a garden. She turned on her side, curled into a ball, and closed her hand around the diamond between her breasts.

Kadar. She imagined the sound of his great wings beating the air, the bright bronze of his hide and hair.

Was it really possible that she'd bewitched a dragon? Or a wolf, when she'd been so powerless that she couldn't do anything more impressive than set herself on fire?

Dragons were wise. Sybil held the stone and wished she could talk to the one who'd given it to her now.

When he spoke, she shrieked and nearly jumped out of her skin. "What have you done, witch?"

"Kadar. You scared the hell out of me." She sat up and blinked at the tall, bronze-haired man who stood in the doorway. He was wearing leather pants, but otherwise he looked exactly the way she'd seen him last. If he was bewitched, wouldn't it show?

"You unnerved a two-thousand-year-old Roman centurion," Kadar returned. "I didn't think that was possible. What did you do to him?"

"Nothing." Sybil pulled the covers up over her breasts belatedly. "He said I'd bewitched all of you, and sent me to my room. I went." She bit her lip. "Is it true?"

He raised a brow at her. "It's true that I adore you and count the days until you come back to me."

She groaned and flopped onto her back, pulling the blanket over her head. "I'm horrible. I'm sorry. I'll find a way to undo it somehow."

"If you think you need to make up to me for some offense, I'm sure I could think of a way." Kadar left the doorway, crossed the room, and sat beside her on the bed. He tugged the blanket down, exposing her bare torso to the waist. She yanked it back up. He frowned at her. "That isn't the way."

Sybil slapped at his hand. "Were you not listening? Adrian thinks I bewitched you. Get away from me. I'm evil."

"If you're evil, I'm the Queen of Sheba."

"Maybe you're overconfident," she muttered. "I could be a Trojan horse. I look harmless, but that thing inside me could be attacking all of you."

"Interesting theory." Kadar won the blanket tug of war and admired her breasts. "Lovely. I've missed those."

"Crazy dragon."

"Fraidy witch." He lowered his head and lapped at her nipples, one after the other. "Adrian is a fool if he doesn't intend to take advantage of these." He closed his mouth over one peak and suckled until she squirmed. He released her and grinned down at her. "There, aren't you feeling better now?"

"Yes. No."

"That's clear. Adrian?" Kadar raised his voice, his head turned back toward the door. The vampire came through it and stopped a couple of feet from the bed. "Watch."

He drew the blanket all the way down to her thighs and levered himself over her, letting his weight rest on her for a minute before he came down on her far side. He faced the vampire with Sybil's body between them. His hand settled on her belly, fingertips brushing the pubic curls that covered her mound. His mouth descended to claim hers in a hot, sweet kiss while he petted her bare body.

His hand skimmed her waist, curved along her hip, slipped over her mound to cup between her legs. Her thighs shifted to allow him to touch more of her, and her breath caught at the realization that Adrian's eyes were following Kadar's hand. Her nipples grew harder and she rocked her hips up to press herself into his palm.

Kadar ended the kiss, rubbed the tip of his nose against hers, and then looked at Adrian. "Do you see it, or are you that blind?"

The other man looked back at him and gave a silent shrug.

"You're a hopeless cynic." Kadar stroked his hand back up to cup her breast. "Get over it. She needs you. Climb into this bed now."

"I'm not the demon," Adrian said. "I didn't invite you over for a threesome."

"No?" Kadar thumbed her nipple, then bent his head to lick it. When Adrian didn't move from his spot by the bed, Kadar stopped his ministrations and looked at the vampire. "If she'd bewitched me, she'd be in control." Kadar's hand dipped between her thighs and she proved how lacking she was in that category when he plunged two fingers into her. She nearly came on the spot. "Why not admit your real reservation?"

Adrian eyed her taut, lust-wracked body. "This seems unfair to her. She may become addicted to me."

"I think she's willing to risk it, considering the alternatives." Kadar withdrew his hand and deliberately licked his fingers. "Good-bye, darling. Be a good girl for the wicked vampire."

"What does he mean, addicted?" Sybil asked, looking up at Kadar through heavy lids.

"He'll explain." Kadar brushed a kiss across her lips, stood, and left her alone with the vampire.

"To mark you, I'll do more than take you with my cock," Adrian stated bluntly. He walked over and sat beside her, the mattress dipping with his weight. "I'll take you with my fangs, too."

She tried not to look faint. It wasn't like she hadn't expected to be a blood donor. She'd just tried not to dwell on the details. "Um, okay. I'm sure there are Band-Aids and ibuprofen if you hurt me in the process."

"It won't hurt." Adrian touched her throat. "Just the opposite. My bite will inject you with my venom. It's an aphrodisiac that induces euphoria. One time may be enough to make you an addict."

She stared at him in silence for a long minute. "First one's free, then you pay forever. Life is such a bitch."

"If you can't accept the risk, I won't touch you."

She sighed. "See, there's a problem with that. You don't touch me, I don't get the full mark." She brought her mouth to his. His lips were warmer than she expected. And hard. "I'm screwed and we both know it, so what's one more thing? Sink fang in me, vampire. I'm yours."

She touched his arm, and his muscles felt like granite. He took control of the kiss, deepening it until her lips softened and clung to his. Then he cupped her chin in his hand, tilted her head to the side, and grazed her throat with his lips. She shivered as he explored the sensitive spot. Then she gasped as he struck. A swift, sharp pain pierced her. Almost instantly, pain exploded into pleasure.

Sybil moaned and reached for him blindly, clinging and arching up under him as he drank from her. Somehow she was on her back and he was half-laying on her. Instead of wondering how things had progressed so quickly, she decided they weren't progressing fast enough. She reached down and tore at his pants.

"Adrian," she groaned. Her sex pulsed and ached and she was going to die if he didn't take her instantly. "Hurry. Please."

He pushed her hand away and got his pants open, freeing his cock. His thighs shifted to press between hers. His body settled fully onto her as she wound her legs around his waist and arched up. "Adrian. Adrian. Now."

His bare chest crushed her soft breasts. His fangs sank deeper. His hips flexed and the thick, blunt head of his cock pushed into her, filling her with himself and a rush of magic. He rocked forward and drove the full length of his shaft home. Her hips bucked wildly under his. Her orgasm hit before he was all the way inside her and continued on and on as he thrust in and out.

The first peak ebbed, built again, and continued to build until she was shaking from the need for release. He took her harder, faster, driving into her until she came a second time. It wasn't enough. The magic building between them combined with the venom coursing through her veins and demanded more.

Sybil made a low protest when Adrian pulled out and turned her over, then cried out at the sharp pleasure as he pushed into her again from behind.

She moved under him in urgent need as he worked his shaft into her inch by inch, chanting his name, sighing when he struck the other side of her neck with his fangs. She could feel his need, and the venom made it ecstasy to let him drink her in. She lost all sense of time, drugged with sex and magic that surged through her in waves while Adrian anchored her body with his.

He slid a hand underneath her and searched out her clit, stroking it as he drove his cock in and out of her channel. The added stimulation sent her rushing to another peak, but this time he joined her. Magic grounded itself in her flesh and burst into the mark she took as he poured himself into her depths.

fifteen

Sybil paced around the room and ran her fingers through her tousled waves, wishing for a mirror. "I think my hair dried funny after what we did in the tub."

"Ronan won't object."

Sybil wrapped her arms around herself and frowned. "Actually, I think he will. I should look proper. Is there a proper look for presenting yourself to an immortal sadomasochistic elf?"

Adrian sat up in bed, giving her a nice view of his muscular arms and chest. "Are you asking me?"

"Yes. You were a Roman centurion. You know about

proper. Also, there are professional designers who don't have your sense of style. Help me out, here."

He studied her for a few minutes, then climbed out of bed, retrieved a carved wooden comb, and went to work on her hair. When he finished, he opened a drawer and took out a white linen shift. He pulled it over her head and adjusted the drape of the fabric. Then his hands went to the catch at the nape of her neck.

"What are you doing?"

"If you want to look like a proper submissive slave for Ronan, you shouldn't go to him wearing jewelry another lover gave you."

The thought of being stripped of Kadar's token sent a wave of panic through her. "I'm not taking it off. He'll just have to deal."

"He's likely to make you deal," Adrian warned her.

"I know. I'm still not taking it off." Although she could think of many things Ronan could do to try to change her mind.

"You are stubborn."

"Actually, I'm pretty damn flexible." Sybil turned around and waved a hand in the air. "I'm making a lot of adjustments, here. It shouldn't all be one way. If I'm prepared to spend the rest of my life being an occasional sex partner to five men I didn't know a week ago without any hope of love, commitment, or fidelity, then a member of a race humans once worshipped as gods should have the grace to let me wear a damn necklace if it makes me feel better."

"You're on fire," Adrian said in a calm, even tone.

She looked down, startled. Ghost flames clothed her and her hair was blowing in an invisible wind, ruining all of his careful grooming. "Oh, crap. That was an accident. I thought I was getting more control."

"You're also a foot off the floor."

"Sorry." Sybil focused on sinking back to earth, and managed a graceful landing for once. The flames didn't lessen. If anything, she burned hotter. "It's not stopping."

"Too much power needs an outlet," Adrian observed.

"I know. I've been channeling it into sex."

"If the past night and day weren't enough, you need a new outlet."

He had a point. "I'm open to suggestions."

"Put it into something. Preferably nothing in my home."

She thought of Abaran and the warning he hadn't taken seriously last night. He might think his skin was Kevlar, but she didn't believe immortal meant impervious to harm. She pictured him in her mind, and then mentally surrounded him with the pent-up force she needed to release. She imagined it clothing him with protection, reinforcing his natural defenses. The fire covering her vanished and she heaved a sigh of relief.

Her hand went to the once-more hopeless tangle of her hair. "Um, Adrian?"

He shook his head at her. "Never mind. As you say, Ronan will just have to deal."

When Abaran didn't appear, Adrian guided her to a meadow full of flowers and surrounded by a ring of oaks.

He took her hand and raised it to his lips. "Thank you for the pleasure of your company. And now I think you'd better wait alone. Ronan will appear when he chooses."

"Like a cat."

The vampire gave a short laugh and left her. Sybil tried not to feel abandoned. Instead, she could take a page from Adrian's book and appreciate beauty. She walked around admiring clusters of orchids in exotic shapes and colors, some like tiny pastel starbursts and others like jeweled bells, breathing in their heady perfume. She leaned against the rough bark of a tree trunk and thought she could feel the stillness of slow growth and roots that ran deep.

She settled on the ground underneath it and looked up at the night sky through the canopy of leaves. When she got bored with that, she practiced flying. When that tired her, she curled on her side in the field of flowers and closed her eyes.

"Rise."

Sybil sat up blinking, and found Ronan standing over her. He seemed taller than she'd remembered, and even more physically perfect. He didn't look amused. Maybe he was insulted that she'd fallen asleep waiting. She got to her feet and tried to brush grass and leaves out of her hair and clothes surreptitiously.

"Follow."

He turned and walked away. Her brows shot up. And she'd thought Kenric was a man of few words. She tagged along behind him, feeling clumsy and slow. He had to be the most graceful being she'd ever seen.

As they walked, the only word she could think of to describe the place he led her to was *bower.* Just past the ring of trees, the greenery grew thick and close together, forming walls and a roof. "*This* is your dungeon?" Sybil blurted out the words before she could stop herself.

He looked at her, his light blue eyes cool. "Do you have permission to speak?"

Her mouth opened in silence and closed with a snap. Then she raised her hand.

"Yes?"

"If I have to have permission to speak or pay the price, you need to tell me the rules. You can't expect me to know what they are by telepathy."

His beautiful head inclined. "You have a point. The rules are simple. You do nothing without my permission. And you accept anything I choose to do."

"Do your other women actually go for this?"

"Yes."

Sybil sighed and rubbed her temples. "You're going to be so high-maintenance. Beautiful people always are."

His mouth curved in a sensual smile. "You are going to be a joy to punish."

"You are going to be a pain in my ass."

"You don't know the half of it." Ronan shook back his silvery hair and strode off. Sybil watched him in awe. From every angle, he was stunning.

"Glamour," she said out loud. "I bet without it, you have bad hair days, too."

He gave her a questioning look.

"Never mind. I'll adjust to being blinded by your glory eventually."

Then she heard music swell from out of nowhere and hardly dared to breathe for fear she'd break the spell of the sound. It was wild and sober, beautiful and terrible, joyful and grieving. It stole her breath and made her heart ache in her chest.

"Come, let us dance." Ronan took her hand in his and began to dance. Since she couldn't do anything else, she followed him. The steps started out like a demonstration of athleticism. Gradually the movements became more like the forms of a martial art. And then more seductive than a tango, raw sex expressed without a word as he drew her closer, skimmed her body with his, turned and lifted her while she floated in his arms.

His lips brushed the curve of her neck where Adrian had bitten her. "You have another lover's mark on your body."

"I do?" She hadn't thought of the vampire's bite that way, but the idea that she had some physical evidence of Adrian's passion on her skin pleased her.

"You do. I will mark you more."

The tattoo. Of course. Sybil nodded and drifted with him, her feet following his, her body supple and light.

"You dance well."

The approval in his voice went to her head. She normally danced like she had two different sizes of shoes and no sense of rhythm. It had to be the music. It had to be magic. Maybe it was Ronan. Whatever the cause, it would never happen again so she reveled in her unexpected grace and the sheer joy of physical expression. "I like dancing with you."

"You know how the dance ends."

She did. It ended with sex. It had to. The steps led inexorably to that, as he directed her and she followed. Surrender, hers to him, theirs to the primal need that sang and beat in all living things.

He drew her down to the earth and onto her back. His hands smoothed the linen shift she wore from neck to thigh, slid under the hem and moved up, exploring the bare skin underneath. His touch felt like an extension of the music. He caressed her with a tenderness that made her throat ache. He explored every nerve center on her body, making her wait until it was agony to be deprived of his hands on her breasts, between her legs. She needed him to touch her there. But he didn't.

Ronan urged her over onto her hands and knees, pushed the skirt up to her waist so she was bare and exposed below it. She waited, anticipating his next touch.

The sharp crack of a cane against the backs of her thighs made her cry out. The second blow, a little higher on her thighs, made her sex convulse. The third struck her buttocks and she groaned at the sensation as blood rushed to the abused area, making it throb, and the delicious sting sent a wash of sensation through her. Her sex clenched again. The fourth blow left her reeling with arousal.

Ronan's hands stroked the rounded swells of her bare butt, slid low. His fingers searched out her core, found her wet and wanting, pushed inside her.

His other hand caressed the curves of her ass before descending in a series of sharp, open-handed smacks as his fingers thrust in and out of her core.

She felt her body draw tight, aching and urgent. She was going to come again. She fought the need to, but the pleasure-pain of his attentions and the partial penetration made her wild.

"Please," she finally begged, spreading her thighs far apart and arching her lower back to offer herself. "Please, Ronan."

When she was teetering on the edge, about to go over it despite her attempt to find control, his fingers pulled out of her.

"Get on your back."

sixteen

Sybil rolled over, panting, her skirt flung up, legs apart, as she stared into Ronan's light blue eyes. Waiting.

He was naked, and he looked like something from the beginning of the world, a primal force. His erection jutted toward her, and she wanted to taste him on her tongue as badly as she wanted to feel him between her thighs.

Ronan lowered himself over her, his hands braced on either side of her. She felt him probe between her legs, hard and hot where she was slick and eager. "Do you take me?"

The formality made her want to laugh, despite the urgent

need thrumming in her body. Or maybe because of it. "With a grain of salt. And do you take *me*?"

For an answer, he pressed forward. His flesh, velvety steel, sheathed itself in hers. Her body opened and stretched to accept him. His torso brushed against hers, above her but not resting his weight on her. The intimate press of him deep inside her made her head spin. The music took on a different note, sang through their joined flesh, and her whole being needed to move to it.

"Dance with me," she whispered.

Ronan's weight settled on her. His long hair fell around her like silver rain, the silk of it against her bare shoulders a seduction all its own. His body intoxicated her. So tall, so sculpted and lean, so unlike any other. Her hands hungered to explore all of him. Her skin yearned for the slide of his, and when he moved on her, in her, she wrapped herself around him and felt her heart leap in celebration.

Wild music played while their bodies merged in the oldest dance. She wanted it to last forever. She wanted to find the release that eluded her. Ronan's pace drew the pleasure out until she was arching up under him, pleading in low, throaty tones, taut and trembling with need. The steady stroke of his flesh into hers was perfection and torment. So much, so good, not enough.

Then it changed. Magic surged and built as the music grew

wilder. He turned fierce, driving deeper and faster into her core in a primitive demand. Her inner muscles tightened in response. She felt herself hang on the precipice, and then the hard length of his cock pushed her over. He pulsed inside her, ejaculating in a hot jet of seed. Her flesh rippled around his in orgasm, accepting, exulting. The music sang in her skin, sound and fire sealing the mark Ronan gave her. He thrust into her again and again while they came together, extending the pleasure, and until finally they came to rest.

Sybil's heart steadied into something slower than a frantic thudding. Her breath came in longer inhalations instead of panting gasps. The weight of him pressed her down, quieting her body, anchoring her.

His lips brushed her forehead. The gesture made her smile. She was still smiling when he drew back to look into her face. She shook her head as the full impact of him struck her all over again. "Seriously, can't you tone it down a little, Ronan?"

He gave her an odd look. "You said that before. Glamour doesn't work on witches. They see through it."

"Looking at you is like looking at the sun," she grumbled. "Well, the moon, at least. Some celestial body." Her hands caressed him, loving the feel of his bare skin and the planes and angles of his form.

"What do you see?"

"Your hair is sort of silver, but it doesn't make you look

old. Your face looks, I don't know, thirty. But your eyes are ancient. Light blue, with those rings around them," she said in a dreamy voice, admiring him. "Your skin is so white it should look pale, but it glows like a star. You're tall, and lean, and your muscles look like the kind made for endurance and not for show. You're so graceful you make everything else look awkward and slow in comparison. I could spend hours just watching you move."

"You sound elf-struck," Ronan said. "But you aren't seeing glamour."

"I am elf-struck. You whipped me." Her reaction to that, the excited urgency and sexual intensity, did not sit well with her. Kadar might've had a point; she was far less disturbed by Ronan's treatment of her than she was by the fact that she'd liked it.

"You wanted me to." He rolled with her, coming to rest on his back with her spilled over his chest, his cock still planted inside her. "You could peak again right now just from the thought of me flogging your naked buttocks."

There was nothing to say to that, so she pressed her cheek against him, needing closeness and tenderness. And when he gave it, that made it worse. His hands were so gentle on her that it made her eyes burn and her throat ache.

I don't want to need this, she thought but didn't say. *I don't want to belong to you when you don't belong to me.*

The final piece that completed the mark signified the end. Ronan would keep her until he chose to let her go or their time ran out, and she would be left to live with the aftermath. None of them were hers. And all of them held a piece of her she would never get back. How long could she stand being an occasional amusement to them when she wanted more?

She couldn't take without giving herself in return. She didn't know how to withhold her heart.

Deal with it, she told herself. *You're alive. You get to have hot, sweaty, mind-bending sex with five supernatural studs whenever they call, separately or in combination. And you never have to pick up their dirty socks.*

It didn't make her feel better, but the way Ronan tied her up did. He bound her hands behind her back with something soft and strong, then had her kneel in front of him while he put a jeweled collar around her neck and fastened a long velvet cord to it.

"Walk with me." The cadence of his voice could seduce her all by itself, she thought. She stood and followed him through oak groves and starlit meadows under twin moons.

Fragments of old poems filtered through her mind. All of them having to do with faerie mounds and time. She'd entered another world on the back of a dragon. She'd been with each of the guardians a day, but how much time had really passed? How many hours had she danced with an elf? How long had she been a wolf's submissive mate, a dragon's prize, a demon's lover, a vampire's source of blood and sex?

Ronan led her back to his bower and tied her leash to one post of an ash bed. Then he tore her shift from neck to hem and stripped it away. He made a fist with one hand in her hair and pushed her down to kneel in front of him. His jutting penis brushed her lips. "Take me in your mouth."

She opened for him obediently and angled her head to allow more of his shaft to thrust between her lips. He tasted of sex and magic. She laved him with her tongue, sucked him deep, felt anticipation coiling tight and low in her body.

His hips worked as he fed himself into her hungry lips. He held her head fast while he spilled himself on her tongue and she swallowed all he gave her.

When he pulled out of her mouth, she saw that they weren't alone. They'd been joined by a wolf and a vampire. It struck her as funny that the sidhe had chosen both the most and the least complicated of her lovers. He'd probably done it on purpose for the contrast.

She ran her tongue along swollen lips, looking from Kenric to Adrian, then up at Ronan, wondering what was next. She didn't have to wonder if they'd enjoyed watching her performance. They were naked and the state of their bodies said it all. She took it as a positive sign that she didn't feel an overwhelming urge to fling herself at Adrian and beg him to pierce a vein. She might be hooked on five lovers, but at least she wasn't hooked on vampire venom.

"On the bed," Ronan ordered her.

Sybil stood up and climbed onto the broad expanse, then sat on one hip with her legs curled beside her. The three of them joined her. Kenric settled on his back. Adrian kneeled at the head of the bed. Ronan took the foot.

It wasn't hard to guess what Ronan wanted her to do, how they planned to share her, but the rules were as easy to remember as the erotic punishment she'd earned already. So she resisted the urge to touch Kenric's body with hers and waited for Ronan to say the words.

"Straddle the wolf and offer the vampire your mouth."

She moved on top of Kenric and wanted to sigh in contentment at the feel of him under her, hard and male, so right, so welcome. She leaned forward and Adrian shifted to meet her. His hand circled the base of his shaft and brought the head of him to her lips. She opened wide and he thrust in to fill her mouth.

Kenric's hands stroked from her hips to her breasts. His palms covered her nipples with pressure she welcomed and arched into. Her sex brushed the hard length of his penis. The contact made her yearn for more. She sucked Adrian with eager lips and rocked her pelvis forward to align her core with the broad head of Kenric's cock.

The two of them petted her with familiar hands. Adrian's tangled in her hair and caressed the curves of her throat and neck. Kenric's teased her nipples into aching points as he pressed slowly, steadily between her thighs.

When Ronan spanked her, her sex tightened convulsively around Kenric's thick shaft and heightened the sensation of being deeply penetrated. Ronan's palm smacked her bare butt repeatedly, making the skin sting pleasurably and arousing her almost beyond endurance.

Kenric's wide shaft filling her pussy wasn't enough. Adrian feeding his length into her greedy mouth wasn't enough. She groaned out loud when she felt Ronan fit his penis, slick with lubricant, between the round globes of her ass. The contact of his head against her sensitized anus made her wild. He began to thrust inside and her body stretched to take him. Inch by inch, he pushed into her tight anal opening from behind while Kenric stroked into her from below and Adrian glided between her lips.

All four of them, joined. All of her filled, taken by three lovers. She loved the fit of Kenric between her legs, the taste of Adrian on her tongue, the dark thrill of Ronan's possession. Most of all she loved that Kenric was there to share the experience and heighten her enjoyment of it.

Adrian came first, a hot rush of salty-sweet fluid she drank down as she continued to suck. She ran her tongue over his head and loved the way he shuddered in reaction. Then she let him slide out of her mouth and lowered her torso to Kenric's. The heat of him against her bare breasts and the musky scent that was uniquely his made her head spin. *My wolf,* she thought, and tightened around him.

Ronan rode her hard and fast. She was stretched exquisitely tight and the ring of delicate tissue he penetrated ached from the sensual delight of his demands.

The counter-rhythm of two men thrusting into her had her teetering on the brink. First Ronan filled her, then Kenric, each pressing as deep as she could take them. Finally Ronan gripped her hips hard and pumped his cock into her ass while he spent himself in short, fast strokes. He withdrew, then Kenric rolled her underneath him.

She looked up at Kenric from beneath heavy lids. His eyes burned gold as he gave her a look of fierce possession that her whole being reacted to. "My turn," he growled.

He didn't look away as he plunged into her again and again. Her hips rocked up to meet his until the force of her orgasm froze her into immobility. Her release triggered his. With their bodies locked tightly together, buried as deep in her as he could go, Kenric's shaft pulsed as he spent himself into her womb.

.   .   .

"I think you enjoyed entertaining my guests, pet." Ronan settled beside her when they were alone again. He curved his palm over the swell of her mound and felt the slick proof of her pleasure with the pads of his fingers. "They certainly enjoyed you."

"Do you guys do this often? Share your women?"

"Never." Ronan stroked his hand up her belly, over the slight rise of her breasts, higher to stroke the sensitive hollows of her throat just below the collar she wore.

Oh. So she offered them novelty value. That wasn't likely to last long.

"Your face is so sad." Ronan pinched her nipple between his fingers, hard enough to get her attention. "Aren't you enjoying your time as my pet?"

Too much. But she struggled to smooth out her expression. "You are the goddess's gift to women."

"Would you like a gift?"

Something in his voice made her frown in concentration as she tried to decode his meaning. He pinched her nipple a little harder and her body pulsed in reaction.

"I'd like to give you a gift for pleasing me." Ronan released her and shifted to unbind her hands. She stretched her arms, then found herself unable to resist the pull of his body. The feel of him under her palms. She touched him with hungry hands, half-expecting him to retaliate with some erotic punishment for her daring.

But his hands on her gave only pleasure, awakening every nerve, plying her with sensual delight. Knowing that could change at any moment kept her on edge, braced for anything. The tension that resulted deepened the intensity of her physical response.

He touched her everywhere. The sensitive hollows at the backs of her knees. The delicate arches of her feet. The nape of her neck. Every touch built on the one before, wrapping her in his spell, until she was drowning in sensation.

The taste of him. The slide of his body against hers. His scent. The light and color and fragrance in the air. The sound of music she almost knew but that at the same time was so strange to her ears that it underscored how alien he was to her.

"What is that song?" Sybil asked, her voice a hushed whisper.

"Listen." Ronan kissed her, a long and thorough melding of mouths that eroded any thought of self-preservation. She could only open to him and offer herself for anything he might want of her.

When he rolled her onto her back and rose above her, she felt a surge of exultation. He slid his legs between hers. His demanding male flesh sought feminine surrender and found it. She was slick and welcoming, easing his entry as he thrust deep.

Flesh mated. Magic pressed her down along with the weight of his body. She smelled demon smoke and fairy flowers combining in some exotic perfume, and wondered if it represented their mingled magic.

Ronan on her, in her, filled her with wonder and hunger in equal measure. He stroked in and out of her, levered himself up so their eyes could meet while their bodies melded, and the sight of him rooted between her legs made her breath stop.

Vines twined around his arms and hers. More wrapped around their hips, binding them together. His white skin took on a green hue. A crown of leaves sprouted in his hair.

Green man. She didn't say it out loud. She couldn't. An ancient symbol of an ancient power, a force of nature. "Is this real?" Sybil found herself asking.

"What do you see?"

"Viridios." She named the Celtic god.

"Witches see through glamour."

Sybil laughed at his answer, amazed instead of afraid. And gave herself to the ancient magic that called masculine to feminine.

. . .

MUCH later she opened her eyes and found herself alone in the meadow of flowers she'd fallen asleep in, waiting for Ronan to appear. She was naked except for a wreath of flowers around her neck where Ronan's collar had been, and where Kadar's necklace still resided. The pendant felt cool and heavy between her breasts. To one side of it, the eight-pointed star inside a circle was complete and stood out in stark relief on her pale skin.

The whole episode might have been a dream, except for the tattoo, the necklace, and the collar of flowers. And the loss of the garment Adrian had dressed her in.

Sybil sat up and rolled to her side, trying to see if her butt and thighs showed signs of Ronan's surprisingly enjoyable form of discipline. Her skin was unmarked.

She settled back into the bed of grass and flowers and took physical inventory. Her body tingled pleasantly in some places and ached enjoyably from exertion in others. All in all, she felt an incredible sense of well-being. Maybe that was Ronan's gift, a surge of vitality. Thoughtful of him.

"If Ronan is really your name," she said out loud. The other name had been his at least temporarily, though. He'd been the green man of legend. That had been more than unexpected.

The whole episode had been filled with the unexpected. The sheer joy of dancing. The shock of discovering she didn't find Ronan's sexual tastes at all unpleasant. He'd cherished her, bound her hands, put her on a leash, ordered her to submit to the orgy, and treated her like a favored mistress.

All of them treated her like she belonged to them. It was like being in some sort of backward harem where instead of many women for one man, there were five men and one woman. She tried to imagine explaining that to anybody from her old life and couldn't.

Not surprising, since she didn't understand it herself.

A sound made her look up. It seemed oddly appropriate to see Kenric there.

"I'm surprised you're not on four feet," Sybil said.

"I'm surprised you're alone."

"I don't think I like your tone. I'm not the one who decided sex with all five of you was the answer." She stood and stretched, displaying her naked body with deliberate insolence.

"Why are you here, anyway?"

"Abaran is missing."

seventeen

A chill went through her at Kenric's stark words. Sybil wrapped her arms around herself. The reflexive action triggered the memory of wings cocooning her in safety. The sense of loss staggered her. Abaran was supposed to be a casual bed partner. Her feelings were anything but casual.

"It's my fault something's happened to him," she said, stricken. Her eyes stung. "I put you all in danger by being here."

Kenric raked a hand through his mane of hair. "I don't have time to listen to you pining for your lost lover. I need to follow his trail, and you need to be watched."

"So I don't go trying anything stupid," Sybil said, feeling her temper rise. She didn't try to tamp it down. Anger felt better than loss and worry.

"That, and so whoever took a guardian doesn't take you, too. You are going to Kadar's cave."

You. The emphasis wasn't lost on her. She might have the mark, but she wasn't part of the team.

But then, what was she?

Sybil walked beside Kenric, matching his rapid strides without effort. "Listen to me. I've been practicing. I can control my power now, and you need my help. It might take all of us together to save Abaran."

"I know you want to help. But you can help best by staying out of the way and under Kadar's protection."

The finality in his tone told her his mind was made up. Arguing with him would be a waste of breath. But Kadar might be another matter. Kenric delivered her and left her seething in frustration.

As soon as he was out of earshot, Sybil turned to Kadar. "What am I now?"

He regarded her thoughtfully. "Who we are is largely defined by our actions. What do you want to be?"

"More than a guardian groupie." She made a gesture. "Not that I see any groupies in residence. But as much fun as the five of you are in the sack, I don't want to be defined by my sex life.

Or who my lovers are. I have the mark, too. Doesn't that make me part of the team?"

"You fill a long-absent part of the team. Once, witches were our allies. I told you before, your power can serve more than your own goals. We need you."

"To close the gate."

"And to guard it afterward, to see that it remains closed."

She looked down at the eight-pointed star. "Kenric made it clear that he wanted me to stay put while he went after Abaran."

"Kenric does not speak for us all."

"Abaran said the five of you didn't want to need me." She touched the mark she wore with a fingertip.

"And what do you want?"

Sybil drew in a deep breath and let it out. "I want Abaran back. I want to go after him."

"Even though you're a target."

She raised her eyes until they met his. "I intend to be a moving target. But I don't want to be the loose cannon that causes a disaster. I want to help, not make things worse. If I'm a member of the team, I should act like one. Not rush off on my own. So let's make a plan."

Kadar produced clothes and handed them to her. "First I'll answer more of your question. What are you now? You're an immortal."

For some reason, that part of it hadn't crossed her mind. "You mean, this isn't just for life, it's forever?"

"We play for keeps in this league." He moved away, stood, stretched, and disappeared into the haze that marked his transformation. When it cleared, a bronze dragon looked at her. "You're an immortal witch holding power coveted on both sides of the gates. By demons in the shadow realms and by a coven in the world you know. You'll have to deal with both. Are you prepared for that?"

Sybil remembered the atavistic fear that had gripped her when black flying things swarmed in the sky. She thought of trusted faces who had been her friends, as close as family, and who might now be the enemy. Who might have been all along.

She finished dressing, drew a shaky breath, and squared her shoulders. "Maybe not prepared, but I'll face whatever I have to. I found the stupid book. I fell under its power. I opened the gate. I'll undo what I did." She would have added *or die trying*, but apparently that was no longer possible.

"Then step into my office." The dragon led the way through the caverns to the world outside. Sybil followed. They emerged into daylight and she blinked at the sight. It seemed like a very long time ago that she'd entered the guardians' realm.

"Just out of curiosity, is that Sol?" She waved at the sun in the sky.

"It is." The dragon's tail wound around her calf like an

affectionate arm. "We're in a magically protected place on Earth. Scientific instruments don't detect us. Humans can't stumble across us."

She snorted. "Explain the poet, then."

"Poets defy explanation. Let's hear you try."

She imagined a stoned Coleridge blundering around the place. How? He'd been in an altered state. . . . "Astral projection?"

"Go to the head of the class."

"Does that sort of thing happen often?"

"No."

Sybil reached out to rub the dragon's flank. "You sound disappointed."

"I used to get a lot of visitors."

"I'll bet." She leaned against him and ran an idle hand over his neck ridges. "Mostly female."

"Yes, but that was long ago. Over time, there was more and more trouble between humans and other races. Then finally there was the great war that removed us from the world and made us guardians of it."

Her hand stilled. "When the witches betrayed you and you died."

eighteen

o *you* trust me?" Sybil asked bluntly. "I have what you were betrayed for. Aren't you afraid I'm going to turn to the dark side?"

"You didn't go looking for power," Kadar pointed out.

"Yes, I did." She stood as tall as she could. "I wanted to wield magic. I didn't want my gift to go to waste."

"The key words being gift and waste. Your intentions were good," the dragon said in a gentle voice. "And you fought being made a tool of dark power, even when you were most helpless."

"Yes, but I'm not helpless now."

"And what do you want to do? Rescue one of our number, and undo the damage you accidentally did. If you were merely power-hungry, you wouldn't care who got hurt."

" 'With great power comes great responsibility,'" Sybil quoted. "That doesn't just apply to Spiderman."

Kadar laughed. "You quote poetry. You get your wisdom from comic books. And you wonder why I trust you?"

"You do?" A smile lit her face.

"And I know another guardian who trusts you, too. If you're ready to go after him, get on." The dragon crouched.

Sybil climbed into position and leaned close to his long neck. "I'm ready."

The rush of air and the rhythmic pumping of wings obliterated any other sound. Kadar flew high and fast toward a ripple in the landscape she could feel before she could see it. It felt cold and wrong and horribly familiar. Demon language whispered in her head and power beat in her veins.

"That's the gate I opened, isn't it?"

"Yes." Kadar dove, bringing them right to the edge of it. "I can't go through. None of us can. Except you. You hold demon magic, so the shadow realms are open to you."

"Abaran is in the shadow realms?" Her mouth went dry and metallic with fear.

"He can be nowhere else. If he was on this side of the gate, we would have found him already."

Of course. Abaran was a demon; if he'd been taken, he would have been taken where he couldn't be rescued. But she could follow him. She drew a shaky breath and slid off Kadar's back before she had time to think about what she was doing. If she thought too much about it, she might faint or run away. "Good thing I've been practicing."

Kadar lowered his head and touched his muzzle to her hair. "Come back to us and bring our brother with you."

"I'll do my best." Sybil hugged the dragon's neck, then turned to face the gate. How did it work? The answer was inside her. She sifted through the book inside her mind, commanding it to give her the spell. The mark of the goddess heated as she bent demon magic to her will. Her hair stirred as heat rose and created a wind. She said the right word as she stepped into nothingness.

It felt like falling, except for the absolute lack of sensory feedback. No light or sound, no sense of her own body's weight or position. The sensory deprivation distorted her perception of time. She might have been on the other side for a few seconds, or much longer.

I want to go back. The panicked thought made something pulse inside her. Ironically, the inner stirring of demon magic calmed her. If she could feel that, she was real, and if she was really here, she had to find Abaran. He'd be looking for his opportunity. What had he said about falling into enemy hands? That he'd use whatever techniques, tactics, and weapons he had. Do whatever offered the greatest chance of success and survival.

He'd be ready. So she just had to find him. They'd handle the rest together.

But how to find anything in this place that was no place? She felt starved for the world of sight and sound, where she was solid and she could touch and be touched. She hungered for it, and the dark magic inside her hungered, too.

Was that all this place was? A place of hunger that could never be satisfied? A prison, where the absence of everything was the ultimate torment? The thought would have made her shudder if she'd felt real enough to have a physical reaction.

But she could feel the tattoo over her heart. She could feel power coursing like molten lava in her veins. Magic was real here. And Abaran's magic resonated like hers.

She pictured tendrils of power snaking out from her, searching the darkness. Somewhere there was a lover, a friend, a partner. If this was a place of unsatisfied desires, maybe she could use that. She needed Abaran.

She needed him, and she sought him with hungry power. Finally she felt him, but couldn't reach him. Sybil probed at the distance that separated them with her magic, stymied. If distance wasn't real here, what kept them apart?

Nothing.

Abaran, she thought. She infused the name with everything she knew of him and the space of all the things she didn't. The mystery of him was as much a part of him as anything she could touch.

Leave me, he answered.

The words filled her head. She would have shaken it in response, but gestures like that had no meaning in this place. *No. I won't. I want you.*

You shouldn't have come here.

But I have. Now let's get out of this place.

She felt his power meld with hers. That was good. Magical contact could be trusted even if nothing else could be. The words she needed formed in her head like letters written in fire. The mark she wore and Kadar's necklace seared her skin as she used the spell to pull both of them to the edge of nothing and out the other side. They erupted into the world of matter and staggered under the weight of it.

"I just twisted my ankle, and it feels so good, I could cry," Sybil panted. Good pain. Welcome pain. Pain was real, and it meant she was, too.

"How did you do that?" Abaran twisted to stare at her in disbelief.

"What, my ankle? I landed wrong. Considering that was my first trip through a gate, I think I got off light." Sybil reached down to rub the throbbing joint.

"How did you find me? How did you free me?"

She shrugged. "I wanted you, and when I found you, I grabbed on. I couldn't at first, so I sort of, I dunno, thought about you. Your name. What you were, what I knew, what I could guess, and what I couldn't even begin to guess. And then I had you. Despite your trying to be noble. 'Leave me'," she mimicked, shooting him a glare. "Like I would leave you to starve forever in that place."

"You summoned me." He looked appalled. "That shouldn't be possible."

"Why? Aren't you a demon?"

"I'm no longer a demon. I'm Inanna's."

"Let's worry about that later." Sybil rubbed her arms. "Do you have any idea how to close this gate?"

"No, but while you're trying to find the user's manual, I'll deal with that." Abaran motioned toward the dark swarm materializing almost on top of them. Sybil shrieked and jumped back. Her ankle shrieked louder but held.

She closed her eyes, since the sight of oncoming death was distracting. Besides, she couldn't actually die, right? "We live through this and the good guys win," she muttered, hoping it was true. Then she looked for the key inside her. If the gate

opened with a demon spell, another should close it. Or maybe
not another; maybe the first spell worked two ways? The difference between open and shut was a swing of the hinge, a
click of the latch.

Words and magic boiled up. She chanted them and prayed
that she wasn't wrong, that she wasn't compounding their
problems by opening another gate.

The spell consumed her, and when she gave breath and
power to the final syllable, it ended and she collapsed onto the
ground.

She opened her eyes and found Abaran busily fighting three
demons. Moments later their forms lay still on the ground, then
evaporated while she watched. "That's just creepy."

"Sybil." He wrapped his arms around her and then she felt
his head jerk up. He swore and before she could react, leathery
wings cocooned her in safety. "Missed a few."

Something struck them. Make that somethings, she realized as his words sank in. More demons. Stragglers left on this
side when she closed the gate.

"Abaran, let go! You're leaving yourself vulnerable!"

"Hush." She felt his tattoo heat and pulse. Power went out
in a shockwave. Then he opened his wings and she blinked at
the dark forms on the ground.

"It's like pouring salt on slugs," she muttered. Her hands

clung to Abaran's waist while she stared at the dissolving demons.

"Don't watch if it bothers you."

"I can't help it." Then she burrowed into his chest and hugged him hard. "Idiot demon, trying to protect me. What if they'd hurt you?"

"Not possible," Abaran pointed out as he hugged her back. His arms were gentle and careful as they enclosed her. "I'm immortal."

"Yeah, yeah, you're Superman." She breathed him in and rubbed her cheek against the leathery skin that was uniquely his. "I'll remember that the next time you're trapped in the shadow realms and need somebody to rescue your ass."

"Mock me again and I'll have to punish you, witch."

"Promise?" She rubbed her body against his, giddy with relief and the sheer delight of physical contact after the voracious emptiness that had swallowed them both. Just the memory of it made her feel starved for sensation. She sobered as she realized Abaran had been trapped there much longer than she had. How much worse had it been for him?

His erection jutted out as if in answer, thick and hard.

Lust flared between them, mixed with the need for comfort and connection, for physical assurance that they were safe and whole. Her nipples pebbled in reaction. "You just want to do it, right here, right now?"

"Right here. Right now. Hard and fast and rough." He stripped her to the waist in one rapid jerk, baring her breasts. Then he yanked her pants down past her hips and made a low sound of approval at the sight of her pubic curls. "No under- wear. Good."

He crouched in front of her and pushed her legs apart. Sybil steadied herself with her hands on his shoulders, and closed her eyes as he dragged his tongue along her folds. She could feel the heat of his breath, the fierce pressure of his lips as he licked and suckled her sex, making her ready for what he needed. When he tongued hungrily into her sheath, she dropped her head back and groaned in pleasure.

The urgency in his mouth, the hard pressure of his fingers as he gripped her bare ass in both hands and held her where he wanted her made liquid heat curl through her. "Abaran."

He licked deeper inside her. Her sex pulsed in response. Just when she realized she really would come first if he kept going a little longer, he stopped, grabbed her waist, and pulled her to the ground. She was on her back and he was over her, between her thighs, his legs holding hers pinned flat as his cock surged into her.

"So wet and ready." He pushed deeper, his angled shaft finding a spot that made her senses sing. It was fast and rough and it didn't last long, but she was already coming when he began to pump jet after jet of heated liquid into her womb. He kept thrusting into her after he'd spent himself, pulling out after he made her come a second time only to roll her onto her knees and position himself behind her.

He entered her again in a slow, steady movement, until he filled her sheath and her sensitized tissues felt stretched to capacity.

She moved with her demon lover and savored the slide of needy flesh into flesh, glad that he wanted to sate himself with her. The wicked angle of his penis delighted her and his open lust stirred hers into something more urgent than willing accommodation. "Harder," she murmured, hips working in restless eagerness with his rhythm.

"Gladly." Abaran's strokes quickened. His breathing sped up to keep pace. So did hers. His hand came around to cup her mound. His fingertips pressed against her clit as he gave a final series of thrusts that sent them both over the edge.

They rested together in a sweat-dampened heap. Abaran made no move to withdraw from her. Instead, he caressed her sex and kissed the back of her neck as they cuddled in a post-coital lassitude.

"Finished?"

The hard edge to Kenric's voice made her scowl as she raised her head. She refused to move away as if she had something to be ashamed of. Instead, she pressed back against Abaran and rocked her hips to goad him. "Why? Did you want to join in?"

"I wasn't talking to you."

Her brows shot up. Abaran stilled and she heard the whisper of wings as they unfurled. "I don't like your tone."

"I don't like finding you screwing your way to oblivion while the witch blinds you to what's happening."

"And what is happening?" Abaran withdrew and stood, lifting her as they rose together so that his arms supported her and kept her close.

"You've fallen under her power. She's using you."

Sybil gaped. "Paranoid much? I know you have a thing about witches, but maybe you didn't notice I just rescued him when you couldn't."

Kenric's jaw tightened. "I noticed that traveling the shadow realm and summoning a demon came easily to you."

"You're saying it was too easy, so I must have cheated?" Sybil realized her fingers were digging into Abaran's forearm hard enough to hurt even his leathery hide and forced herself to relax her grip. "It couldn't possibly be because I'm good for something besides a wild time in the sack?"

"Sybil." Abaran's voice carried a low warning.

She looked down to make sure she wasn't floating. No. Feet firmly on the ground, and no phantom flames, either. She was getting it under control, she really was. Even though she was so furious she was almost shaking. "I'm okay." She looked at Abaran and was startled by the cold, faraway look in his eye.

"It was too easy," the demon said.

"Don't tell me you're getting as paranoid as the wolf. You were there. It was horrible and scary and after we got out, you had to fight the demons that were on this side while I figured out how to close the gate. Was that easy?" Disbelief made her voice rise.

"It was too easy." Abaran's sober eyes regarded her in silence while a cold chill crept over her.

"You're serious."

He nodded.

"Hell." Sybil bent, found her scattered clothes, and dressed in record time. "Okay, now what?"

The question wasn't addressed specifically to either man, but it still surprised her when Kenric answered.

"Now we destroy your coven before you join with them and hand Abaran over to them."

Before she could process that, let alone respond, Kenric aimed a wave of power toward her. It washed over her and carried everything away.

nineteen

Stupid, stupid, stupid. Sybil cursed silently while she struggled to orient herself. Stupid not to see it coming. Stupid not to defend herself. Stupid to feel like crying because a werewolf didn't trust her and never would.

Under the roiling emotions, though, came a sense of wrongness that grew sharper as she found it impossible to determine where she was. If Kenric had knocked her on her ass, was she sprawled on the ground? Upright? It shouldn't have been hard to figure out. But it was.

A horrible possibility dawned. What if nothing since entering the gate had really happened? What if everything else was just made of shadows?

Abaran. She thought his name and filled it with intent, feeling for him. There. The unmistakable signature of her own strange power mingled with his, the result of her attempt to burn off the excess and reinforce his protection. If she ever got out of here, she needed to thank Adrian for suggesting she aim it at something outside his house.

I told you it was too easy.

He'd said that to her right before Kenric struck her down.

So that really happened?

Yes and no, he replied. *You found me, but the rest of it? Battling shadows. It was an illusion.*

Well. That sucks. Sybil would've kicked something, but lacked a solid target.

Yes, it does. Abaran's complete agreement came through clearly in his mental tone.

So where was the real exit? What was the key?

"You know the answer," a low female voice replied. The voice sounded like hers, but oddly distorted. Like hearing herself on a recorded message. Sybil blinked as a mirror image of herself strode toward her out of the mist. Except she'd never looked that confident or together in her life. Or that dangerous. Shadow Sybil had eyes that burned with cold fire and a presence that crackled with power.

"Who are you?"

"Your shadow."

Right. Her shadow self. Sybil dug into her mind frantically for some scrap of knowledge that might prove useful. She focused all her energy on tapping into the deepest recesses of her magical reserves. What was the shadow? Something to do with choices. The opposite created by decisions taken or not taken.

"So, what, I'm supposed to do battle with my own shadow?"

"Or you could just let me win." Shadow Sybil smiled coldly and raised upturned palms that crackled with blue flame.

She was her own worst enemy. Sybil fought the urge to laugh and dodged instead as a fireball shot toward her. "Missed me."

"That was a warning shot." Her shadow self moved closer, bathed in flame from head to toe.

"Maybe. Or maybe I'm faster." Sybil danced back and set her own power free. It was easier here. The demon magic inside her was very much at home in this realm. But she didn't return the strike. Engaging in direct combat might not be the smart thing to do. If she battled her own shadow, would she destroy a part of herself?

If the shadow was the person she'd chosen not to be, did that make it good, bad, or a mix? All bad implied that she'd always made the right choices.

"You're my psychic twin," Sybil stated, stalling for time while she thought furiously.

"You wish you looked as good as me." Her shadow curled a contemptuous lip.

"Well, obviously you reflect my choice to spend more time living and less time in front of the mirror." Sybil cocked her head. "I think I made the right call."

"You also chose to be weak."

Another blast nearly struck her full force. Sybil blocked it with a matching burst of power, the two cancelling each other out. "I'm not that weak."

"Then why don't you stop me?" Her shadow swept closer and Sybil shifted away.

"Maybe stopping you isn't the right choice." It was then that the knowledge bubbled up in her consciousness. Since she couldn't destroy her shadow self, she had to embrace it and make herself whole.

"Whatever choice you make, I'll oppose."

"For every action, there's an equal and opposite reaction," Sybil agreed.

"You choose delaying tactics. I choose a strong offense."

Her shadow attacked a third time. This time, instead of blocking or evading, Sybil moved into the attack and flung her arms around her shadow opponent.

The impact staggered her. Power met and merged, so much of it she couldn't possibly remain the conduit for it for long without being consumed.

"I embrace my shadow," Sybil whispered or shouted. She couldn't hear anything over the roaring in her ears. "Good and bad, I own what I am."

In answer, a column of energy ate her.

"Sybil. Sybil. Witch, answer."

Two leathery hands gripped hers. The sensation was both exotic and familiar. "Abaran?"

"You know me. You live."

The relief in his voice made her summon the strength to open her eyes. "We can't die, remember?"

"Under ordinary circumstances, no," the demon agreed. He looked haggard and tense. "You encountered the full manifestation of your shadow and merged with it. Even I didn't dare try that."

"Merged?" She licked her lips. "Does that mean I won?"

"It means you lived to tell the tale, and you won our freedom." He lowered his forehead to rest it against hers. "You aged me a thousand years in the process."

"I've always liked older men." She almost smiled but caution killed the response. "How do I know we're really out this time? This could be another mind trick."

"You are a creature of both realms. Judge for yourself."

Sybil sat up slowly and looked around. There was the gate; she felt its distinctive energy signature. There was the place she'd slid from Kadar's back; she felt the trace of him that remained where he'd touched the earth. The web of worry lines on Abaran's face didn't strike her as things of illusion. The signs of his sojurn in the shadow realms altered his appearance subtly. In their earlier shared illusion, he'd looked exactly the same as he had before.

"You look like I feel," Sybil said, raising a hand to cup his cheek. "That seems more realistic than the two of us defeating an army of demons and then feeling good enough to get it on."

"You wound me," Abaran said but with too much relief to put much conviction into his protest. "I only need to see you to be inspired to new heights of sexual excess."

She let out a short laugh. Then she turned her attention back to the gate. "It's the same, but different. Is it closed?"

"I'm not sure what you did to it, to be honest." The demon sat back and studied her, his face unreadable. "You grabbed your shadow self, and then took both the gate and me. For lack of a better description, I'd say you possessed us."

"I don't remember." She remembered wanting out, and taking a desperate gamble that would either save them or turn out to be a really, really bad idea. "If it worked, though, we can call it a success. Then we just need to close that thing."

"Be my guest." He waved an inviting hand toward the topic of discussion.

Sybil loosed magic, shaped it to her will, and probed the gate. It wasn't just shut, it was sealed. "Huh. Why do I get the feeling I could do the demonic 'open sesame' chant again and it wouldn't open this time?"

"I implore you not to try."

His dry tone made her smile. Then she frowned in concentration, tracing the gate with power and intent, feeling the change in it. It was sealed. She rose and moved closer to it, testing. She tried to probe beyond the barrier with a cautious toe, then her hand. It remained impenetrable.

"I can't pass through," Sybil said, turning to look at Abaran over her shoulder. "You try."

When it failed to allow Abaran to pass, she let her knees sag in relief. "Well, that's done."

"So are you, I think." He slid an arm around her waist and pulled her against his side, offering support. She took it gladly, absorbing the welcome physical proof of his presence at the same time. He felt warm and solid and safe. She could have collapsed in relief for those things alone. Their escape from the shadow realms and the safely sealed gate were almost too much to take in.

"The mighty heroes return victorious," she sighed. "Can we go home now?"

"In a moment." He tucked her more securely against his side and rubbed his cheek against the top of her head. "Do you remember who we met after our shadow victory, and what happened?"

"It's not the kind of thing I could forget." Sybil shivered. "Kenric blasted me. Accused me of conspiring with the witches to turn you over to them."

"I think his shadow delivered a message to us."

"Hell." She felt a chill creep through her. "I didn't need him to tell me they're up to something. But what would they want with you?"

"The same thing they want with you. Power they hope to take and twist to their own ends."

But the coven didn't want a demon, they wanted the lost book. Didn't they? "If they want to turn the world into chaos, I don't see how getting their hands on you would help."

"Then you don't realize what I am yet?"

The question made her suck in a breath as she saw it. "Oh. The last of your kind. You're the last chaos demon."

It made sense. They resonated magically because the power she'd unwittingly absorbed had the same base as his.

"I don't understand," she said, pulling away to look into his face. "Kenric said your kind fought on his side. Why, if you were the ones who made the damn book?"

His dark eyes met hers. "Chaos needs order. Balance. The book was never meant to leave the shadow realms. The lost word was meant to stay hidden. We sealed it away so it would remain forever unspoken."

"But the rest of the demons wanted to destroy what was

on the other side of the gate," Sybil said slowly. "Or maybe they thought they'd create a new order. One that put them on top. So they conspired with the witches."

She didn't have to ask why. Hunger, an eternal gnawing appetite for more. The visceral memory of that hungry place would remain with her no matter how many centuries she lived beyond this day.

"They nearly succeeded."

"Twice," Sybil agreed. "Let's not go for three." The coven had to be stopped. Abaran had to be kept far from their reach. And she was the one they wanted.

She knew what she had to do. She drew on the mark they both shared and the demon power they both carried and slowly, surely, recited the words that sent him away. Then she pointed a finger at the ground, carved symbols in the earth with raw power shaped according to her desire, and stepped into them.

"what do you mean, you lost her?" Fury blossomed in Kenric's midsection as he spoke. His voice was taut with that emotion, each word spoken as if bitten off.

Abaran's jaw unclenched enough to let him answer. "She was too fast. I didn't guess what she would do until she had me locked in a sending spell."

Kenric rounded on the dragon. "You sent her after him alone."

A bronze shoulder shrugged indolently. "I could hardly follow past the point his trail led. Of all of us, only she could."

"Of course she could. She's chock full of the accumulated power of an entire race of demons. That doesn't explain why you thought it was a good idea to send her on a rescue mission with practically no training or experience. It's a miracle they aren't both still trapped there."

A pointed tail flicked in a sign of irritation. "She's clever and she has good instincts."

Kenric turned back to the demon. "Let us recap the order of events. The dragon, in his wisdom, sent Sybil to drag you back to this side of the gate and close it. She managed, against all reason, to do this. And then a skinny little slip of an apprentice witch boxed you up and shipped you home while she headed straight into a trap. Have I got that right?"

Abaran's teeth grated audibly. "Yes."

"You realize they have what they want now. What they've wanted from the beginning." Kenric's voice took on a growling, lupine timbre as he spoke.

"I wouldn't be so sure they have the book," Kadar said. "Our little witch has a formidable will."

"Formidable." Kenric wanted to rend something. "She can't defend herself against an organized assault from a united coven trained in magical arts. Even if she wanted to, she couldn't keep what they want from them."

"Even if she wanted to?" It was Adrian who repeated the phrase and made a question of it. "Whose side do you believe she's on? She was a victim of the book, not a willing sacrifice to it. She prayed to the goddess for aid, and accepted the form that took. She accepted us. She accepted the mark. She risked herself to retrieve one of our number from beyond our reach. Then she sent him beyond the reach of his enemies. Why do you still doubt her loyalty?"

"I doubt her loyalty, her sense, and her sanity," Kenric snapped. "She just handed over everything that coven has conspired to gain."

"She's strong enough to withstand their attacks," Abaran said.

"Then why do you look worried?" Kenric countered.

The demon's wings unfurled. "She's alone."

Abaran's words made Kenric's veins freeze as he realized that under the heat of anger was cold, cold fear. She was so fragile. She could be so easily hurt, while he was too far away to help.

"Not for long." Wolf, dragon, sidhe, and vampire spoke in unison.

twenty

If the set of *Macbeth* collided with Donald Trump's board-
room, Sybil thought it would look something like the
scene before her. Eleven women who looked more like
executives than crones gathered around a cauldron, in a room
with sober paneling that could've been installed in any office.
The lack of windows made the room feel oppressively close.
Black candles occupied strategic positions and emitted an oily
smoke that tainted the air. The arcane symbols covering the
parquet floor made her skin crawl. It was a weird mix of every-
day and otherworldly.

She'd grown up dropping in and out of this house with

complete freedom, always welcome. She'd never seen this part of it before. It was a little like going into a neighbor's house you thought you knew as well as your own and discovering the hidden room with evidence of bizarre sexual rituals, violent crimes, or both.

If she'd entertained any doubts that this coven was black, they were laid to rest now.

"What's for dinner?" Sybil asked, lounging in the doorway with deliberate nonchalance. "If it's eye of newt, I think I'd rather get take-out."

"Hello, Sybil dear," Maxine said. The smiling grandmotherly face didn't hide the avarice or cruelty that gleamed in her eyes. How had she missed that all this time? "You won't mind eating what's in the cauldron. Although it does have a powerful aftertaste."

"Sounds interesting." Sybil channeled her inner shadow and pretended to consider the bubbling pot. "I take it you're not serving revenge. I hear that's best cold."

Maxine laughed, a silvery sound that perfectly fit her appearance and contrasted sharply with the lack of humor in her eyes. "Revenge is such a limited goal. We think in broader terms."

"Much broader," Ginny agreed, turning to nod at Sybil while she continued to stir the noisome concoction. "It's a night for dreams to take flight."

"Or nightmares," Sybil said. "You've been planning this for ages, haven't you? To wipe out humanity and claim dominion over the human realm."

"Long past time," Ginny said as she ladled out a portion and inhaled the steam like a dedicated chef. "Needs more rat."

"We're glad you've come to us. It makes things so much easier," said Susan, a comfortably rounded woman in her forties.

"So much easier," echoed Maxine. "I told you banishing and binding the demon would lead her here."

"What's a demon got to do with it?" Sybil examined her nails, projecting boredom, making sure the fire that burned just under her skin remained invisible.

"You and demons share such a strong common interest now." Maxine laughed her bell-like laugh again. "We felt the gate open. You can imagine our delight when we found the spell's signature coming from your apartment. At last, you've fulfilled your ancestral destiny." The woman positively beamed. "You're a living demon grimoire."

"It's a shame you won't survive the process of removing it," Ginny said. "You're going to miss all the excitement."

"And the glory." Susan's eyes shone with fanatical light. "We'll all be in our glory."

Sybil resisted the urge to tell her that was probably spelled without an L. Instead, she tightened her control on the demon power that lay ready to erupt and extended her focus to the tattoo that pulsed against her skin. "Sounds fascinating. I'd hate to miss it. I mean, I've already missed so much. Growing up without a mother, for starters."

"This is precisely why you don't deserve to have the book." Maxine frowned at her. "You think small. You could be focusing on the big picture. Instead, you want your petty revenge and completely ignore the opportunity you have. You could have an army of demons at your command. You could rule on both sides of the gate."

"I like to keep things manageable," Sybil said. "Ruler of realms? Sounds like it would really suck up my free time."

"You lack vision. You also lack a certain necessary ruthlessness."

"I wouldn't be too sure about that." Sybil might be newly acquainted with her ruthless side, but already she could see the potential benefit. *Me and my shadow.*

"I hate to say it, but you're also a foolish girl." Maxine's grandmotherly frown of concern fell short of creating the proper impression. "You came right into our place of power. You're ours now."

"You're wrong. I'm Inanna's and she really doesn't like what you're cooking."

"Inanna? Old days, old gods, old powers." Maxine walked

toward her. "It's a time for new gods to be born. And time for you to die, dear."

"I don't think so." Sybil let flames sheath her and drew on the multi-pointed star. The cauldron shattered and white heat burned away every trace of the potion. Tendrils of power imprisoned each coven member in a hold as invisible as it was unbreakable. But she stopped there instead of increasing the pressure until it reached lethal force. Killing didn't seem like the answer here, anymore than it had when she faced her shadow self.

Goddess, what do I do with them now?

Let them face their own shadows.

Perfect. Sybil reached inside herself, found the key to the sealed gate, opened it, and sent her captives through before sealing it again behind them.

She managed to make it outside the room full of wrongness before she collapsed. She still had enough reserve to seal the chamber and drive the internal temperature up until it erupted in fire.

Then she rested on the floor and listened to the distant wail of sirens and wondered how long it would take some nice paramedic to come and help her to her feet. Of course, it was probably a bad idea to let one find her at the scene of the crime, no matter how nice he was. But getting up was beyond her. So was activating another spell. She'd never drawn on so much of her power in such a short span of time, and it nearly depleted her.

Fortunately, the dilemma was solved for her when a large, black wolf appeared. The wolf became a man and then she was lifted up by a strong pair of arms.

"Just in time," she murmured, curling into him. He hugged her hard and she felt him bury his face in her hair for a moment, as if breathing in her scent. She rested her cheek against his chest. She wanted to stay there forever, listening to the rhythmic thud of his heart, pretending it beat for her.

"Did we miss all the fun?" Kadar peered down at her over Kenric's shoulder. "Weren't there some wicked witches to deal with?"

"There were. But since they thought it was such a good idea to bind Abaran in the shadow realms, I thought they should see for themselves what that was like."

Abaran's low laugh made her raise her head and turn toward the sound. "Are you all here?"

"One for all, and all for one." Kadar spoke for them.

Sybil took in the sight of Ronan and Adrian and felt something inside her unknot. The guardians were a team and they'd moved as a team to join her. The five of them together still stole her breath. Each man gorgeous and formidable in his own distinctive way. As a group, the cumulative effect of male beauty, brawn, and unmistakable power packed a wallop.

And they were all her lovers. That either made her one lucky witch, or one who was in way, way over her head.

It was Ronan whose words chilled her blood when he spoke. "Demons incoming."

She felt Kenric's muscles bunch as he turned to assess the threat. The movement gave her a line of sight to the sky through the window. It was filled with dark-winged creatures.

"Won't people notice that?" Sybil imagined a rash of phone calls reporting the invasion to local news sources and a War of the Worlds–style hysteria spreading.

"No more than they see the wind. You can tell where it's been and see the results, but the force itself is invisible," Kenric answered.

She struggled to slide from his hold. "Put me down. You'll need your hands free. If I can't be an asset in this fight, I can at least not be a liability."

Kenric set her on her feet. "Return to Xanadu. Wait for us there."

"No." She might still be too spent to be much help, but if she could be any help at all, she needed to be present to give it.

His face hardened. "You said it yourself. You can at least not be a liability." He touched the eight-pointed star on his chest. It glowed with power. She felt her own pulsate as if in answer. A heartbeat later, she was standing unsteadily in Kadar's lair.

"Dammit." She sagged against a rock wall. Then she kicked it. The sharp pain that shot up her leg from the impact of her heel made her grimace.

Sent home to wait and twiddle her thumbs while they dealt with the remaining threat. That said volumes about what Kenric considered her strategic advantages; she had none.

Not knowing what was happening made her pace restlessly. Her exile chafed. If she was part of the team, shouldn't she be with them? After all, she didn't just have demon magic, she had Inanna's mark and the reinforcing strength of her shadow self.

At the same time, the use of so much raw power had left her weak. Just the effort of pacing had wiped her out again. Sybil gave in to trembling limbs and sank down to sit with her back resting against rough stone. Since she didn't have much choice, she'd sit this one out. Next time, it'd be a different story.

The enemy came at them with the desperate fury of a force whose retreat had been cut off. The demons brought war and the guardians met them head on.

Kenric leaped and snapped, tearing with powerful jaws and teeth, bringing down one demon after another as he overpowered them with sheer muscle mass, striking vulnerable points with well-aimed bolts of power. The five guardians formed a loose ring with their backs to the center and by ones or by groups the enemy fell to them.

Kadar fought in dragon form, sweeping with his tail, rending with his claws. Abaran moved like a dark shadow, now here, now there, striking without warning. Ronan danced with his sword and felled every demon who partnered him in his bloody ballet. Adrian fought with quiet power and focus, choosing his targets and watching for his opportunities.

Kenric grinned at the next demon who rushed him, meting out death with joyous ferocity. This was what they were made for. They guarded the mortal world that never knew its own peril or suspected the form of its salvation. Unseen, unheard, unknown, they watched and when needed, they fought.

Purpose drove him. Discipline sustained him. Immortal, unceasing, unstoppable, he carried out his duty until no more enemies cast themselves into his jaws and the Shadow Guardians were surrounded by piles of steaming, stinking demon carcasses.

"It's finished," Adrian said.

"Abaran and I will sweep for stragglers." Kadar gathered himself, preparing to launch into flight. "If you hadn't sent our other flying member away, this would be good training for her."

Kenric didn't answer. He didn't deny that her abilities could prove useful, and since she had them, common sense demanded she train them to serve her. But the easy way the dragon called her their other member disturbed him.

She was one of their number in a sense now, yes. Made so by chance and circumstance. But would she fight beside them? Could he trust her at his back if she did?

"She saved Abaran and defeated the coven," the dragon said, reading his thoughts. "As for how she came to bear the mark, did any of us plan this life? You don't want to trust her. As long as you hold her at arm's length, you don't have to face what she is to you."

With that, he sprang into the sky. Abaran unfurled his wings and followed. They split off, one taking the east, the other the west. Kenric watched them dwindle to invisibility in the distance.

Twenty-one

Kenric found the witch dozing with her cheek pillowed against cold stone, like a sentinel who'd tried and failed to stay awake through the watch.

She hadn't bathed or changed. Her face was still pale from exertion and the hollows beneath her cheekbones accentuated her fragile appearance. If not for a certain softness in her expression as she slept and the bold sparkle of the diamond contrasting with her utilitarian clothing, she might have been a female mercenary. But there was that betraying softness about her. And she wore her lover's token openly.

Men of war became familiar with two sorts of women.

There were camp followers, and there were those who were warriors in their own right, who'd cut down any man who dared lay a hand on them. This woman fit neither group.

She fought like a warrior, albeit an untrained and undisciplined one who would benefit from hours of practice. She abandoned herself to pleasure with her five lovers, then set out to rescue the one of their number who had gone missing as if he was her comrade in arms.

A camp follower had many lovers, but looked to her own interests. A warrior female looked to the interests of her comrades but had no lovers.

But then, she was a true witch. Witches had always been a law unto themselves. It had been such a long time, he'd forgotten that.

As if she'd sensed she was watched, her eyes fluttered open. "Hello, wolf. I take it the demons have been defeated?"

He padded closer and nudged her with enough force to dislodge her from her uncomfortable seat, but gently.

She yawned, stretched, and rose to her feet, wincing as she straightened. "Ouch. Shouldn't have gone to sleep like that."

No, she shouldn't have. A soldier knew to sleep when the opportunity came, to keep himself sharp for action. And knew better than to do it in a position guaranteed to make muscles stiff instead of ready. But as Kadar had said, she was clever. She'd learn quickly enough.

He turned and made for his own bed, trusting her to follow. She stumbled along in his wake. He heard her yawn more than once. His blankets must have seemed as inviting to her as to him, since she curled into them before he'd finished arranging himself for rest. He kept his wolf form. He didn't want a sex partner tonight. He simply wanted the witch where he could keep an eye on her. If there was another reason he desired her presence, he didn't choose to examine it. Kadar's accusation surfaced in his head. Ruthlessly, he buried it.

Her fingers dug into the thick ruff of fur at the back of his neck. "This is nice," she mumbled on the heels of another yawn. "I've never had a dog."

After a beat her hand stiffened, then carefully withdrew. "I mean, I think a dog would be nice. Not that you are. Or that you're mine."

Her awkward retraction amused instead of annoying him. He pretended sleep. She gradually relaxed beside him. When he heard her breathing deepen, he allowed himself to follow suit.

She made enough noise in her sleep to rouse him repeatedly through the night. She tossed and turned, mumbled, cried out once. Then she shifted closer and quieted as if she found his nearness a comfort. That kept him awake long after she'd slipped into a deeper, undisturbed sleep.

. . .

sybil woke up to an empty bed and a sense of unreality as disorienting as her hopefully never-to-be-repeated trip to the shadow realms. If there were any other witches in the world, she couldn't sense them. She knew what to look for now, the power signature was unmistakable. The coven had masked theirs, but not well enough to fool another witch. She had known them for what they were before she'd gone into their secret room.

As she lay in bed thinking back on the previous day's events, she was haunted by a niggling question. Would Kenric find an excuse to exclude her the next time there was trouble? Would he ever be able to accept her as part of the team?

Well, one way or another, she'd find out. But there was nothing to gain from worrying about it.

She took a walk in the underground woods to clear her head. Exercise helped. It forced her to take deep, steady breaths, to find a rhythm, to ground herself. She didn't meet any of the others. After a while, she found herself at Adrian's doorstep. She suppressed a grin, wondering if a vampire could block her from its home once she'd been invited in.

He didn't answer her knock, so she decided not to test the theory or invade his privacy. Instead, she made her way around to a courtyard garden marked off by low stone walls. A bed of herbs filled the air with lemon and lavender. Olive trees and a grape arbor created shade. Flowers and neatly staked rows of vegetables bordered a lush swath of lawn. In the center of the grass, a fountain bubbled inside a ring of stone benches. Adrian stood facing the fountain with his back to her.

"Hello."

He didn't answer, but turned and extended a hand in invitation. Sybil came forward and took the hand he offered. He clasped hers in a sure grip and drew her closer to his side.

"This is beautiful," she said after they'd stood together in silence for a few minutes.

"As are you." He raised her hand and brushed his lips across the backs of her knuckles.

She laughed. "I slept in my clothes and we both know my hair is impossible."

"I still find you a bright spot in my garden."

"There's an easy explanation for that." She leaned into him. "You probably need a donor after yesterday. Anything with hemoglobin would look good to you."

"Perhaps I see you with affection and would find you lovely in any case."

"Perhaps." Sybil was willing to accept the possibility that the feeling she had for him was returned in some fashion. She liked Adrian. She found him compelling, attractive, and strangely restful company. They'd shared blood, sex, and magic. Was it so hard to think he might like her, too?

"I don't think you came to visit just to see if I was in need of a donor, as you put it."

"Mmm. No." She pulled her hand free of his so she could wrap both of her arms around his waist. "I came to say thank you."

"To thank me?" Surprise colored his voice. Adrian's arms closed around her, returning her embrace. "For what?"

"It was your idea for me to aim excess power at something. I sent it into Abaran, and it helped me find him in the shadow realm. I promised myself I'd thank you for that if we ever managed to get out."

"Luck."

"Somebody once said we make our own," Sybil returned. She pressed closer, taking pleasure in the feel of his body against hers, his masculine frame a delightful contrast to her feminine.

"Careful. Anything you offer me, I'll take." Adrian's voice took on a thickened note.

"Take what you like."

"What I like." He echoed her words, then buried his face in the curve of her neck. "What I like is to puncture your sweet flesh with my fangs while I pierce your body with mine. What I like is to drink from you while you shudder with pleasure. What I like is to know I can have you again and again."

"Sweet talker." She grinned and tilted her head further to make it easier for him to find the vein.

His teeth grazed her skin. She made a low sound of delight. He raised his head to look into her eyes. "Are you truly here because you wish to be? Or have I enslaved you with venom?"

"You've enslaved me with kindness, great sex, and exquisite taste," Sybil assured him. "The venom is a rush, but honestly, I'm just glad it makes something you need a mutually enjoyable act. I was prepared to do it because I was prepared to accept whatever being your lover meant. But I'm glad it's not something I just endure or hope you won't need from me too often. This way is much better."

"Much better," Adrian agreed. He took her mouth, kissing her until her head spun and her body felt fluid and soft. Then he undressed her with unrushed movments and stripped away her clothes one item at a time.

Sybil returned the favor, unbuttoning his shirt and pulling it open to run her hands over his bare chest and abdomen. He shrugged out of the open garment and let it fall, then lowered her naked to the ground. The grass cushioned her back, soft and smelling of sun and green life.

Adrian moved over her, sliding her legs apart with his, holding his weight above her as he nuzzled her throat, then moved lower to lave her breasts with his tongue. He closed his mouth over one nipple and drew on it, the suction sending a wave of sensation through her that made her hips move in restless need. She reached for him and buried her fingers in his hair, holding him there, arching her ribcage up like an offering.

He rolled her nipple in his mouth, then let it slide free. Sybil made a soft sound as the cool air struck bare skin still damp from his tongue.

He turned his attention to the other tight bud, drawing the peak of her breast into his mouth, flicking his tongue over her nipple, then sinking his fangs into the tender flesh. Venom sent her into a delirium of pleasure as he suckled. Her arms tightened around him and her head thrashed from side to side. She wound her legs around his thighs and tried to draw him closer, lost in urgency.

"Adrian," she groaned out loud. "Hurry, please."

He released her and raised his head, heat flaring in his eyes. "Not too fast." He kissed the valley between her breasts, moved down to feather his lips along the soft skin of her belly, scooting back on his knees between her open legs to close his mouth over her clit.

The heat of his mouth and the suction he applied to her sensitive flesh nearly made her come out of her skin. His tongue explored her folds, licking and suckling as if she tasted like his favorite candy. Her hips rocked up to meet his mouth and her breath became a panting moan.

"Now," Adrian murmured. He worked his pants down his hips and left them that way, lowered just enough to free his thick penis. He settled into the cradle of her hips, guided himself into position, then thrust all the way inside her and struck the side of her neck with his fangs simultaneously.

Sybil wrapped her legs around his waist, opening herself wider to take him deeper. Her hard nipples rubbed against his chest as he rode her. His fangs pierced her skin with sweet pleasure. His shaft filled her again and again, each stroke sending her further into a white heat of ecstasy that finally burst in a series of orgasms that rolled through her, one after another. He drew her pleasure out, then spilled himself into her as they peaked together and drifted slowly back down.

Afterward, they exchanged a series of lazy, thorough kisses flavored with a tang of copper. Adrian raised his head and looked into her face. "I have never been thanked so delightfully in all my long years."

"You're welcome." Sybil smiled at him, feeling sated and unreasonably good from the vampire venom coursing in her veins.

"You look drugged."

"I'm not complaining." She smiled wider.

"I should get off you, or you'll have reason to complain later."

"I won't complain later, either."

Adrian laughed. They rested together in a tangle of limbs, and Sybil felt something like contentment mixed with the sexual buzz. Eventually they got to their feet and pulled themselves together. Then she tried not to wreck his garden while he showed her through it, explaining the uses and benefits of various plants.

Restlessness returned. After a leisurely good-bye kiss, she left Adrian to his solitary peace, glad he'd shared a measure of it with her.

She made her way back to what she thought of as "the wolf's woods" and found the wolf himself lounging under a tree. He stood when he saw her, his warrior's body a feast for her eyes.

"They have this new invention," Sybil said in a grave voice. "Maybe you've heard of it. They call it clothing."

"I call it an annoyance to be avoided whenever possible."

"It probably is a real pain in the ass for a shapeshifter," she agreed. "So many potential problems. How do you carry them around when you're in animal form, how do you keep from damaging them when you shift. If I were you, I'd probably just give up and stay in the buff, too."

He scowled. "It is not giving up."

She spread her hands. "Not trying to pick a fight. And not complaining when it gives me such a great view."

"You enjoy the sight of my body?"

"As if you didn't know." She shook her head. "It's distracting, though. I see you naked and suddenly can't remember what I was thinking or doing."

"What have you been doing?"

"I went to visit Adrian."

Kenric moved closer. "I smell him on your skin. You must have enjoyed the sight of his body as well."

"Yes."

"Did he please you?"

"Very much."

"I'll please you more."

"I don't doubt it."

He gave her a hard kiss that made her breath catch, backed her up against a tree, and sent his hands roaming over her body.

"You don't mind?" Sybil asked when she get enough air to speak.

"That you enjoy your other lovers? I find it arousing. I like the sight of you flushed from sex. I like seeing you under another man. I like sharing you, seeing how much pleasure you can take. I find the competition for your favor stimulating. Which of us can please you the most?"

"I don't think of it as competition," she said, blinking at the thought. "I mean, not in the sense of all of you competing for me. More like, I can't compete since I'm not in the same league."

"You're in our league now."

"Am I?" Suddenly sober, she tilted her head back to meet

his eyes. "Am I in your league? If I hadn't been exhausted yesterday, would you have sent me away, or expected me to take my place with you?"

A frown darkened his face. "That's a foolish question."

"I don't think it is."

"You have no training, no discipline, no experience."

"Then I'd better start getting some." She stared back at him without blinking.

Kenric took a step back and let his hands fall away from her. His eyes held hers in silence for a minute that felt like eternity. Then he spoke as if choosing his words very carefully. "Your place is not in battle."

A giant fist closed around her heart and squeezed. Despite everything, despite all she'd done and risked, he couldn't or wouldn't see her as a part of the team. He wouldn't even open enough to tell her why. It hurt so much she went numb inside.

"Then my place isn't here." She let the fire rise to dance over her skin, stirring her hair with the wind created by its heat. "I stand with all of you, or I stand alone."

His jaw tightened. "You're overreacting."

"I don't think I am." She rose into the air and hovered a moment, saying good-bye with her heart. "I'm not the one who betrayed you. When you decide you can trust me, come and find me. I might still care."

Twenty-Two

And they say you can't go home again," Sybil said out loud, looking around her apartment. It felt unlived in, abandoned. She hadn't been gone that long. But then, she'd packed a lot of living into the time she'd been away.

It felt strange to be alone. Stranger to know that she wasn't in an underground cave system that ran according to magical rules. She felt out of sorts, out of synch, and being home just made it worse. This place should feel familiar. She should feel like she belonged. Instead, she felt like a time traveler studying the past.

Okay, then, she'd get out. See some humans. Mingle. Maybe

she'd even take one home with her. That thought made her heart wrench and her stomach tighten.

But as Sybil glanced around the silent living room, she decided that staying there alone, remembering how she'd first met Kenric, wasn't exactly a good mental health move.

She took the time to shower and change into something she hadn't worn through a battle zone, then headed for her car.

Driving wasn't nearly as fun as flying, but the muscle memory and habits that took over made her feel more human. Putting on the seatbelt. Disengaging the parking brake, engaging the gear. Sybil made her way to a bar she'd heard the name of frequently but never been to before. Maybe she'd feel less strange in a place she didn't know.

Parking and locking the car were automatic. She made her way inside, found an empty spot at the bar, and ordered a draft. It tasted wrong, but that's what she got for drinking what was on tap. Sybil pushed the glass to one side and focused on the crowd.

Human faces. Human sounds. Human dramas. A couple in the corner kissing. More on the dance floor flirting, touching, leading up to an inevitable conclusion. The atmosphere seemed sexually charged, from the music to the low lighting. All around, people were hooking up. And she was alone. Sybil took another sip of her beer and wondered why this had seemed like a good idea.

"Come here often?"

The lazy masculine voice made her turn her head. The man who'd asked the question leaned against the bar beside her. He was attractive, and the half-smile on his face told her he knew it and gave the accident of genetics a lot more credit than it warranted.

If he ever met Ronan, his ego would shrivel up and die.

"No," Sybil said. Her tone, expression, and body language added *go away.*

"Want to dance?"

"No." She turned back to her beer. Ronan looked better and danced better. Mere mortals couldn't compete.

"Want to leave?"

She swung back to stare in disbelief at the question. "No." Heat prickled under her skin as power gathered. "I like it here."

"Waiting for a better offer?" The man smirked at her. "Good luck."

He left. Sybil brooded. She had five better offers waiting. She just didn't know what to do with them. The one thing she knew for certain now was that she didn't belong here anymore. This wasn't her world.

You can't go home again. But if home wasn't an option, what did that leave?

She could go back to Xanadu. She could hole up in Kadar's

lair and let him run interference for her with Kenric, but that seemed both cowardly and unfair. She was a big girl. She should fight her own battles, not lean on a dragon. Okay, then, go back, choose her own place. Maybe Kenric couldn't accept her, but he couldn't throw her out, either. Over time, she could outwait his stubbornness and wear him down.

And why did she want to wear him down? She forced herself to face the question and answer honestly. Because she did care. Because she'd been drawn to him from the beginning. Back at the oasis, she'd known it wasn't smart. She'd wanted him anyway. And then she'd given herself to him and that had sealed the deal.

For her, at least. And he wasn't indifferent to her. But if he couldn't trust her, they had an unsolvable problem.

Too restless to stay, Sybil retrieved her car and drove back home. Was there anything in her apartment she wanted to take with her? She wandered through it, idly touching books, pictures. None of it seemed real to her anymore. Nothing seemed to belong to her.

Maybe she was just tired. Big decisions like what to take and what to abandon could wait until morning. At least here sleeping alone should feel normal. Sybil retreated to her bedroom, stripped, and fell into bed. The space around her seemed empty. She hugged her pillow, curled into a ball, and closed her eyes.

The heated skin against hers might have been a dream. The hands that pulled her closer, the low growl, blended with memory and fragments of night visions. Sybil turned into the warm male body that held her and nuzzled the strong column of a familiar throat.

"Kenric." She might have thought the name or said it out loud.

"Witch." The word sounded almost anguished. The tone disturbed the drowsy pleasure she felt, sending a rift through the dream of contentment in his presence. His hands tightened on her, and his jaw rubbed against her hair. "You left."

"You didn't want me." Her sleep-thickened voice was matter of fact.

"I want you."

"For this?" Sybil hooked her leg over his.

"And more." He levered his weight onto her and pushed her into the mattress, his body hard and heated as it settled between her legs and on top of her torso. "You belong to me."

"I belong to all of you, and none of you are mine." She woke up all the way, but not in time to gather her defenses. The ache in her heart echoed audibly in her voice.

"I am yours." Kenric rested his forehead against hers. "Is that what you wanted me to admit? You hold me in the palms of your little hands."

She blinked, confused. This sounded like a dream, but it felt real. "Kenric?"

He growled again. "Who did you hope would come after you? Did you want your pet dragon? Your beloved demon? The vampire who broods over you? The fae who lost his head for the first time in a very long life?"

Sybil took a shaky breath. "I didn't think any of you would come after me. Not this soon."

"They all wanted to come. I claimed the privilege. I claim the right. I claim you."

Her world tilted. Her heart leaped. "What?"

"You heard." His mouth slanted over hers, hard and demanding and utterly welcome. "You're mine. My mate."

She kissed him back until the voice of reason made her break away. "You don't trust me."

"I trust you. You were right, you aren't the one who betrayed me."

"You say that now, but what about the next time something makes you doubt and you look at me and only see a witch?"

"Witches are a law unto themselves," Kenric answered. "I trust you to be true to your own law, and to us."

"And the next time there's an open gate, a loose demon, or some other threat to the mortal world?"

"I won't try to keep you safe, far from the action." The words sounded grudging. "I forgot that you're immortal, too.

My head knew it, but my body wanted to be between my mate and any danger."

"Has your body learned its lesson, or do I need to teach it one?"

"I need many lessons."

Sybil laughed and undulated beneath him, loving the press of his body against hers. "Then we should get started right away."

"I will devote myself to study."

Kenric lowered his mouth to hers, claiming her lips, persuading them to part for him, and exploring with his tongue. She drank in the taste of him, twined her tongue with his, and wound her arms and legs around him to hold him closer.

His hands moved over her, discovering sensitive places to exploit and seducing her with every touch until nothing was left but a soul-deep longing to join flesh to flesh.

Kenric aligned their bodies and entered her with a single, slow thrust, drawing the moment out as she stretched to accommodate him. The sensation of his shaft filling her, pressing further in until she held all of him, sent waves of urgent heat through her. Then the knot formed, deepening his possession of her.

He drank her groan of pleasure from her lips. Sybil strained to get closer, to take more of him and offer more of herself. His body on hers, in hers, felt like a gift and a miracle. Each stroke sent need spiraling inside her, need drawing her muscles taut, her sheath gripping him tight, then rippling in orgasm. His rhythm sped up, and then she felt his cock jerking inside her. The heated liquid jet of his release heightened her pleasure. Their movements slowed as they rocked together, drawing it out before they came to rest, spent, flesh still locked together.

when he was able to, Kenric rolled to his back and pulled his woman with him, tucking her securely into his side. She'd taken his heart with her when she left, and he hadn't even known he'd lost it until then.

"What changed your mind?" Sybil traced the outline of Inanna's star on his chest as she asked the question.

"A dragon threatened to brain me if I didn't get over my stupidity."

"Nothing else?"

"Let's see. The elf said he understood if I didn't feel worthy of you, but since he'd been a god, he could be your equal."

Sybil laughed. Kenric didn't. The sidhe had meant it, damn him. "The vampire said I had spent too much time with whores and not enough time in the company of women of quality and it had rendered me incapable of appreciating you. He himself had no such liability."

"Adrian is a gentleman."

"The demon thought I was insane for allowing you to get away. He would have ended the argument by sating you with pleasure until he'd driven any disagreement from your mind."

"Fighting is probably foreplay to Abaran," she said. "But nice as all this is to hear, it doesn't really answer my question. Somehow I don't think you went around having heart to heart chats with all the guys to explain why I wasn't there, leading to the sudden realization that you couldn't live without me."

"Of course not. They knew the moment you left and descended on me to drum enlightenment into my skull by way of their fists if need be. They blamed me for driving you away. They were right."

"Did they enlighten you by way of their fists?" She rose up on one elbow, peering at him as if searching for evidence of violence.

"They didn't have to. I had a fist-sized hole in my chest the moment you left me. And a matching hollow place in my gut when I realized what that meant."

"Chest pains and hunger pangs. It must be love," Sybil agreed in a solemn voice.

"Joy at the sight of you," Kenric corrected, reaching out to trace her features. "Peace at your presence, close by in the night. A host of emotions, some pleasant, some painful. All of them better than the hollowness left behind with you gone."

She brushed a kiss against the corner of his lips. "Did it really make you feel at peace to have me sleep beside you?"

"Yes."

"When you were still in your wolf form?"

"Enjoying your presence is not always sexual. It feels right to have my mate nearby, wrong when you are absent."

"Does that mean you missed me after you handed me off to Kadar?"

Kenric settled her slight form atop him and wrapped his arms around her, securing her there. Her little nipples pebbled against his chest, and he could feel her sleek thighs and the outward curve of her pubic mound right where he could make use of them. "I missed you. You might remember that I joined you when the opportunity presented itself."

"Threesomes and foursomes, oh my," Sybil said with a soft laugh. "Which reminds me, Abaran said I should ask you what the knot meant. It was on my to-do list, but between getting possessed by a demon grimoire, demon battles, rescue missions, and a bunch of wicked witches, it slipped my mind."

His arms tightened around her. "It meant I was an idiot. I told myself it wasn't possible, you were a witch, you couldn't be my mate. But from the first time, my body knew what you were to me."

"It's a mate thing?"

"It's a mate thing." He brushed his lips against her hair and struggled for words. "Something I never thought I'd have. You thought I didn't trust you. I told myself I couldn't trust another witch, but the truth is, I didn't trust myself. I was the alpha. It was my duty to protect my people. I was the one who failed. If you were my mate, I had to face the fear that I might fail to keep you safe. So I tried to keep you at arm's length."

Kadar had been right about that. If he'd listened to the dragon sooner, she never would have left.

Sybil was quiet for a minute, absorbing his words. "That makes a twisted kind of sense. I hope you're over it now."

"I think I was over it about two seconds after you left me."

"Good." She nuzzled him, then asked, "What about the others?"

"If I don't bring you back, they'll put my immortality to the test," he informed her in a dry voice.

She giggled. "Not what I meant. I mean, you and me, and the others. I'm your mate. I think I felt it from the first time, too, but they're still part of this."

"I enjoy having you to myself, but I also enjoy having you with others. We are going to need a much larger bed." Kenric felt his balls tighten at the thought of her naked body stretched out on a very accommodating mattress, with him between her thighs and two other men on each side of her. Just thinking of it made him achingly hard.

"I like it, too." She slipped her thighs over his hips. The

change in position opened her and brought her slick labia into contact with his cock. "Especially when we're like this. It's amazing how quickly I adapted to multiple partner sex and how deprived I'd feel if I couldn't have two men at once ever again."

"I think they will all do their best to ensure that you are never deprived." Kenric slid his hands down to cup her buttocks, molding them in his hands, then pulling her down a bare inch so that his head penetrated her folds. "But when we're alone, I can go as hard and fast as I please, without having to take care not to jar you or upset another's rhythm."

"So we're good either way," Sybil said with a sigh. She arched her back and pushed against him, taking another inch of his shaft inside. "I want you to understand that it isn't just sex, though. Kadar said I'd be a junior wife to all the others if one of you claimed me, and that's how I feel. I care about each of them. I didn't just go to Adrian to have a quickie spiced with venom. I like his company, and I liked learning about his garden."

"That doesn't mean you love me less." He thrust deep without warning, seating himself fully inside her. "I understand that."

"You have what you want, then." Her inner muscles quivered and tightened around his invading shaft. Her hips made tiny movements, rocking just enough to feel the pressure of his full penetration at the deepest point. "I'm a tiny bit in love with each of them, but I love you with a passion that's unreasonable."

"Show me your unreasonable passion," Kenric invited with a guttural growl.

"Like this?" She undulated on top of him, teasing him with her small, perfect breasts, gliding up and down his thick shaft with her slick, hot flesh that parted readily for him and enclosed him so tightly his breath expelled in a hiss.

"You make me feel very unreasonable when you do that." His voice roughened. His hands gripped her hips, giving him leverage to thrust a fraction deeper.

"If we have this, I'm not sure there's any point to reason." Her breathy whisper caught as he rocked his pelvis into hers.

"You will get no argument from me." Instinct gripped him now. His mate rode astride him, and the time had come to claim her with pleasure.

He established an irregular rhythm that kept them both on the edge, teetering on the brink of fulfillment. They were locked together until their release, a moment he brought closer and closer, then denied them both. He loved the smooth slide of her bare skin against his, the subtle perfume of her skin, the softness of her hair, the wet heat that drove him wild.

"Mine," he whispered, claiming ownership of her body and her heart. "You're mine. No other lover gives you what I do."

She made an inarticulate sound. Then to his surprise her tiny, sharp teeth raked his shoulder. "You're mine," she returned, her voice low and fierce. Power crackled along her skin as ghost flame danced. "Mine until the end of time."

That struck him as just possibly long enough. He moved harder, faster, taking her with urgent need.

twenty-three

Hours later, Kenric carried his sleepy mate to Kadar's opulent bed, drew back the covers, and settled her between them. The dragon man trailed after him, watching.

"Bringing me a gift? How thoughtful."

Kenric bared his teeth in a mock-ferocious grin. "I don't come to give but to take. You have the largest bed."

"I hope you don't think I'll leave it to you."

"You'll notice I put her in the center." Kenric climbed in on one side. "There's plenty of space for us all."

"All?" The other man took the open side and wasted no

time sandwiching the sleeping witch between them. "Have you invited more company?"

"No, but they'll be here anyway. They'll want to welcome her, and she deserves a proper mating celebration."

Kadar nodded and spoke the formal words. "Joy to you both. Joy of your hearts, joy of your bodies, and may the sharing of your joy increase it beyond measure."

"Joy to you, brother of my heart. Share my joy in my mate." He'd always thought the old ceremony would fade from memory, never used. Now a mate had come and the five men were no longer solitary guardians. They had a lover and wife to cherish, and a powerful new ally in their eternal duty.

"Do you want to share her between us?"

Kenric shook his head. "I want to watch her joy in you."

He watched as the other man cupped her face with tender fingers, kissed her with sensual expertise until she responded, her mouth softening and parting for his, then finally opening for his tongue to sweep inside.

His witch. His woman. Her nipples pebbled in reaction as Kadar caressed them first with skillful fingers, then lavished attention on them with his mouth until they bloomed like exotic flowers, darkened and dampened from suction and pressure.

Kenric took in the picture of sensual abandon she made, her eyes half-lidded and her body relaxed with her legs a little apart. He bent to kiss her sweet mouth, running his tongue along her lower lip before sliding it inside, enjoying the way Kadar's devotion to her breasts made the act of kissing hotter, more erotic.

He drew back to allow the other man to slide on top. Sybil's eyes held his, dark with passion and alight with emotion. "I love you."

"And I love you." He caught her hand and twined their fingers together, sharing the moment when her body opened to accept Kadar's, the steady press that seated that exotic cock deep inside her, the flush of pleasure that spread across her cheeks and reddened her lips. Watching her was nearly as satisfying as having her himself.

Her eyes closed as she gave herself up to the moment. Soft sighs and moans escaped her as she moved under Kadar and with him. Her legs wrapped around the dragon's back, and she laughed when he tickled her with his tail. Then the laugh turned into a groan as Kadar thrust deeper, his tempo increasing.

"So beautiful," Kenric murmured. "The sight of you giving yourself to him makes me ache to take you all over again."

"You'll have to wait," Kadar said. He stroked in and out of her as if luxuriating in her body. "You were right, the others are already on their way."

"Others?" Sybil's eyes opened wide, looking to him for explanation.

"I've claimed you as my mate. They'll come to welcome you and celebrate with us, sharing in our joy as Kadar does."

"Five men in one bed. I'm not sure we'll all fit."

"We'll manage." Kenric brushed a kiss against her forehead and noted the tension in her body, the fine tremors that wracked her and the way her breath came shallow and fast. "You're so close. Let Kadar give you everything you want."

"I want . . . oh. That. Yes!" She panted and then bucked and twisted under her lover, keening her pleasure as she came in a frenzy.

"Yes," Kadar growled in response. He pumped faster and then came with a roar as the other three men joined them and formed a loose ring around the bed. "I'm fucking you while they all watch. Coming in you."

She squealed and peaked again, spine bowing. "Little exhibitionist," Kadar added with a laugh, kissing her as they came to rest.

"Lucky for me, you like to show off." She kissed him back with obvious enjoyment.

He withdrew from her reluctantly, then lounged against the pillows at the top of the bed. He fondled her breasts while she lay in naked abandon.

"Joy to you both. Joy of your hearts, joy of your bodies, and may the sharing of your joy increase it beyond measure." Adrian, Ronan, and Abaran spoke the words in unison.

"Joy to you, brothers of my heart. Share my joy in my mate."

"This is actually sweet," Sybil murmured. "I didn't expect sweet when I joined a group dedicated to a sex goddess."

"She's a warrior goddess, too, don't forget." Kenric kissed her as the demon, vampire, and sidhe arranged themselves around her. "In the face of war, we should celebrate sex as the symbol of life and savor the sweet."

"Wise." She opened her arms to embrace the demon first, exchanging a deep, heated kiss. Then she took Adrian's hand between both of hers and bared the curve of her neck in invitation.

"You should decide how you wish to join with us first," Adrian rasped out. "The venom may make you forget yourself."

"You underneath," Sybil said after a moment of consideration. "Me on top, Abaran from behind. Ronan after the three of us finish."

They shifted to take their places. Adrian settled her legs over his hips, then drew her down until her breasts rested on his chest. His fangs caressed her neck, then struck.

Kenric watched her back arch and her body tighten in pleasure as the vampire drank from her and pumped venom into her bloodstream in exchange. Adrian wrapped a hand around the base of his thick cock and guided it to her willing opening. He pushed into her an inch at a time as her body accepted him.

Abaran curved himself over her back, covering her as if to express his desire to cherish and protect. He kissed the back of her neck and then down the line of her spine, feathering a kiss on the dimple that marked the base of her spine and the beginning of the rounded curves of her buttocks. He drew his penis along the line that marked their separation, then pressed the head against the tight, puckered opening between.

"Abaran," she murmured in throaty encouragement. "Yes. I want you."

Adrian released her neck. Sybil turned her head to smile at her mate. Kenric returned her smile, and bent to kiss her as two men shared her between them and doubled her pleasure in the act.

The two of them took her with a lusty abandon that made her body arch and quiver in response. Adrian brought them both to the peak first, and then Abaran brought her to a second peak as he penetrated her from behind.

Abaran withdrew and moved aside. Adrian claimed a final kiss, his flesh still pressed deep into her. Then he withdrew also while Kenric lifted her clear and settled her into the center of the bed again.

"Ronan alone, or the both of us?" Kenric asked, gazing into her pleasure-dazed eyes.

"Both, please." She smiled at him, her lips a lush curve of female softness that seduced him.

"How?" He smoothed a strand of her hair back.

"However Ronan wants. He needs to be in control."

The sidhe laughed. "Clever witch. I'll tell you what I want, then. Raise up on your knees and pleasure your wolf with your mouth while I take you from behind both ways."

"Creative," Sybil said.

Then her mouth took Kenric while the sidhe took her, thrusting first into her slick sex, and then into her tight anus after he'd ridden her to orgasm. He brought her to pleasure one last time, and Kenric shared in the moment, spilling himself as he thrust between her lips, her throat working as she swallowed him down.

"Now what?" Sybil asked the question, looking around the bed at the sprawl of sated bodies.

"Now we sleep." Kenric settled her against his side. Kadar claimed her other side.

"All together?"

"The bed's big enough."

"Barely," Kadar said, mock concern thick in his voice. "We need to conserve space. Scoot closer." He spooned up with his groin nestled against her bare butt, making her laugh.

Kenric felt her small hand burrow into his. He felt something in his chest tighten at that tiny, trusting gesture. His.

. . .

The group ate together late the following morning, serenaded by birdsong. Sybil kept trying to identify the call of one particular bird, following avian shapes until her eyes strained. Then she stiffened. "Tell me that isn't what I think it is."

Kenric rose to stand beside her, following the point her hand indicated. "Demon. Incoming."

"I guess the honeymoon's over," she snorted. He felt the tension in her, and recognized it as the twin to his own surge of anticipation. She practically quivered with the need to engage the enemy.

"It will never be over," he assured her. "This is just a brief interruption. Ready to fight beside me?"

She turned to meet his eyes, her expressive face alight. "You mean it? No 'witches can't be trusted' business? No 'leave the woman behind so she won't be a liability'?"

"You've proven yourself an asset in combat," Kenric admitted. "And you bear the mark. You are one of us. You share our honor and duty."

"I love you." Her eyes darkened. She kissed him hard enough to make him take a surprised step back, then whirled to orient herself to keep the demon in sight. Flame engulfed her.

"Possibly as much as I love you," he answered.

Then six Shadow Guardians stood to meet the threat.

"An author who never leaves you wanting—
except maybe for her next book."

—*Romance Junkies*